# A Different Kind of Valentine

### The Witness
K.J. Dahlen

### The Prize
C.L. Kraemer

### Crazy 'Bout You
Clay Renick

### Time Changes
Nicolette Zamora

Published by Rogue Phoenix Press
Copyright © 2009
ISBN: 978-1-62420-304-6

# The Witness

K.J. Dahlen

# Chapter One

Colton glanced out from under the rim of his Stetson hat as his horse picked his way through the snow storm. His slicker kept him relatively dry, but the air was saturated with dampness. Colton gazed at the darkened sky frown wrinkles creasing his forehead. After such a dry summer and fall all this snow wasn't doing anyone any good. The ground wasn't frozen enough to allow the snow to stay. A couple of days and the snow would melt and leave behind a mess of mud and mire unless the temperatures dropped drastically.

Colton had been working this morning checking line fences. His ranch was home to about one hundred fifty cattle. He was out checking his fences to make sure his cattle stayed within the boundaries of his property. There was a chill in the air. Glancing at the skies he knew the storm wasn't over yet. Winter could be harsh in Minnesota but it wasn't here yet. This, he knew, was only the beginning; even though it was December he knew January and February could be worse.

He nudged his horse to the edge of the creek watching the waters as they swirled and rushed past him. He saw ice crusting around the edges, but with the depth of the creek and the fast paced current, the creek wouldn't freeze until much later in the season. Because of the dry summer and fall the water level was down and Colton was worried. This stream weaved its way all over the property. His cattle needed the water it provided to survive. From the corner of his eye he caught the sight of something that didn't belong in the water. It was a small shoe. Colton frowned and slid off his horse. Reaching into the water he grabbed the shoe and hauled it out of the river. Looking at it, he found it was a woman's tennis shoe. Colton glanced around but didn't find anything else in or around the water that didn't belong there. Grabbing the reins of his horse he began walking upstream. Around the bend of the stream he found the wreckage of a car that had come off the road above the creek. The car had come to a sudden stop against a tree beside the water. The car was a small dark blue sedan and the driver's side bumper was crumpled as it rested against the clump of trees. Colton could also see some damage to the back passenger side panels. He wasn't sure what caused the damage in the back but could hazard a guess. He quickly glanced up the embankment and found a slight indent of the path down the hill the car took. Snow had covered some of the indent and that told him the accident happened sometime during the night. One of the doors was open and there was a young woman slumped in the front seat.

Colton made his way over to the car and checked the woman's condition. She had a nasty cut on her forehead and when he touched her neck for a pulse, she frowned and tried to stir but couldn't. Her skin was pale except for the cut on her forehead. He glanced at the windshield and found a spot where her head met the windshield. The oval impact area was marked by a spider web effect in the safety glass. Her skin was cold and damp and Colton knew he couldn't leave her here. Another couple of hours and she could freeze to death. She was dressed in black jeans and a blue sweater but she wasn't wearing a jacket. He glanced down at her feet and found she was only wearing one shoe. How she lost the other shoe in the creek was anybody's guess. All he knew was her body temperature was dangerously low and she needed his help.

He gathered her into his arms and carried her over to his horse. She wasn't very big and she didn't weigh more than a hay bale. He lifted her easily. Knowing he had to get her warm in a hurry, he draped her in front of the saddle then mounted his horse and adjusted her body to fit the curve of his own. When he thought she was secure, he gathered the reins and turned his horse toward home.

He led the horse to a two-story farmhouse that had been standing there for almost a hundred years. It wasn't until he carried her to the house she began to waken. She groaned and fought against his hold. Colton had to tighten his grip or drop her, and that's when she pushed against him harder. He tightened his hold. Opening the back door he walked through the kitchen and living room to his bedroom and laid her gently on the bed. He turned to look at the fireplace in the corner of the room and found the embers of the fire he built last night were nothing more than a few glowing embers. He quickly added a few more pieces of wood and soon the fire was burning again.

He turned back to his guest to assess the situation. Knowing he had to get her warm again he covered her up with a heavy quilt then he went to the bathroom for a washcloth. Her forehead had dried blood caked around the cut, and he needed to see how badly she was hurt. When he came back, she hadn't moved.

Her hair was a deep shade of red and pulled back into a ponytail. Colton couldn't see how long it was; the tail part of it was tucked behind her back. With her eyes closed he couldn't see what color they were but he'd bet they were green. Her face was heart shaped and her face was pale. He began bathing the bruise. Gently cleaning the dried blood away he found the cut wasn't as bad as it could have been. When the cut began bleeding again, he stopped and applied pressure to stop the bleeding.

She groaned and tried to turn away but he wouldn't let her. She tried to open her eyes but the effort was too much for her. Colton decided to let her rest. He went outside to take care of his horse.

Half an hour later as he was walking from the barn he paused and watched as a dark blue car drove up his driveway. He'd recognized the car immediately as belonging to Sheriff Grayson Trainer. Grayson stopped his vehicle beside Colton and stepped from the car. Grayson was a shorter man than Colton, but he considered himself a better man because he wore the uniform of sheriff.

Leaning against the car he nodded to Colton and pushed back the hat on his head. His blonde hair was cut short. His eyes were hidden behind aviator's sunglasses. His face was tanned from being outdoors all day long. "Good morning Colton."

Colton nodded but didn't return the greeting. "What can I do for you Grayson?" Colton asked politely. Grayson had reminded him on earlier occasions that he preferred to be called Sheriff, and Colton knew it but he refused to give him the prestige that came with the office. He didn't like Grayson and Grayson knew it. The two men had grown up in the same town and theirs was a long time dislike of each other. Colton considered Grayson a bully and over the years that hadn't changed.

Grayson's lips tightened for a moment. His hands twitched briefly as if they wanted to curl into fists. Grayson held his breath then exhaled deeply as he remembered what he came for. "I received a bulletin from the police over in Coven Glade. I was asked to let all the area farmers know about it. The police asked me to be on the lookout for a woman. She would be a stranger to these parts, and she's wanted for questioning regarding a murder." Grayson stood and adjusted his belt. He brushed his hand over the butt of his gun and watched as Colton's eyes were drawn to his weapon.

Coven Glade was a good ninety miles away, but it was the closest big city around. While most of the immediate area was farmland, the nearest small town was Benton, population 753. Benton wasn't very big but it sported a post office and several small shops and a couple of bars. You could get a haircut in Benton and get a screwdriver at the local hardware shop, but for any big purchases or a week's worth of groceries most of the local people went to Coven Glade.

Colton thought about the woman he had rescued, but he kept his thoughts to himself. "Sorry, I haven't seen anybody around here."

Grayson took off his sunglasses and glared at him. "If you see anyone you don't recognize, call me immediately. This woman would just as soon shoot you as look at you." His eyes narrowed and he looked as if he wouldn't mind doing that himself.

Colton raised an eyebrow. He knew the idea of shooting him had given the other man some hint of pleasure. "Why is that?"

"Like I said, she's wanted for questioning in a murder investigation. She's armed and wouldn't hesitate to shoot to get away. She's also wanted for ripping off drugs and money from the crime scene." Colton got the feeling Grayson tried to make the woman out to be more than she was to shock him into helping find her.

Colton's expression didn't change. He simply looked at Grayson, waiting for the other man to finish his business and leave. "What's this dangerous woman's name? What does she look like, in case I run into her I mean?"

Grayson's hand brushed against his gun. He looked as if he wanted to smash something. Taking a deep breath he told Colton, "She's a small woman with dark red hair and her name is Betty Morgan. That's all I can tell you right now." Grayson got back into his car. He glared at Colton through the window as he put his sunglasses back on. "If you see her, make sure you call me. Like I said before she's a dangerous woman, and I know how to deal with the likes of her. That is my job, dealing with criminals, you know."

Colton simply looked at him. He watched as Grayson's car drove down the long driveway. When he turned right onto the highway, Colton glanced toward the house. He didn't want to think about what Grayson would have done if he had told him about the woman he rescued this morning. He realized he might be harboring a criminal, but he needed more information from her before he would decide what to do with her.

Colton climbed the steps of the house and strode inside. The wind had picked up. It was blowing the cold in from the north and Colton could feel the bite of it. He had a feeling the temperatures would drop soon bringing with it more snow tonight. It wasn't the time to get caught outside.

Colton checked the wood-burning stove, adding a couple more chunks of wood before he glanced at the partially closed bedroom door. He knew he should check on his inconvenient visitor to make sure she was all right, but when he opened the door, he found the bed empty.

He stepped further into the room. Panic set in when he didn't find her right away. He glanced over at the window, but the window was closed against the cold outside. He went around the far side of the bed and found her there. She was lying on the floor tangled in the quilt. She was unconscious and her head wound had started bleeding again.

Colton picked her up and carefully carried her over to the bed. He laid her on the bed. She groaned and tried to push him away from her, but she didn't have the strength to put up much of a fight. She tried to get up again but couldn't. She fell back against the covers and tears fell down her cheeks as she whispered "Ian."

Colton frowned. She didn't seem like the murderer Grayson said she was. He could see a gentleness in her that didn't fit with the type of person Grayson Trainer told him she was. He hadn't quite figured her out. He laid the back of his hand on her face and noted her skin was still cold to the touch. He frowned when she turned her face into the curve of his hand. He got up to get her another quilt. When he wrapped it around her, he watched as she snuggled down into its warmth. Cole watched her. He couldn't help but wonder what happened last night that brought her into his world. Was it fate that brought her to him or was it something else? Doubt slipped into his mind when he remembered Grayson's warning. This woman was wanted for possibly drug dealing and murder. From his point of view something just didn't add up.

Colton moved over to the chair watching her sleep for a while. There were too many questions that needed answers—he was determined to get them before he decided what to do with her. He got up to put some more wood on the fire. When it was crackling again he glanced at the window. The wind was still blowing hard. It was blowing the snow around outside and Colton knew this woman had been very lucky to be found when she was. She would have frozen to death.

# Chapter Two

She was finally getting warm. When she realized she wasn't trapped in her car but wrapped up in a warm quilt, she tried to open her eyes. Her head hurt like the very devil, but she knew she had to wake up.

At first she couldn't focus. Everything around her was fuzzy. Feeling a moment of anxiousness she closed her eyes then opened them again. Panic set in when she didn't recognize the room she was in. Nothing around her was familiar, not even the quilt giving her warmth. She struggled to sit up. The movement caused her head to throb. Loosening the braid to ease the pain, she fought back the urge to throw up. When the room finally quit spinning, she glanced around slowly. The room looked like it belonged to a man. She could see the wardrobe in the corner of the room. The doors didn't quite close; there was a red flannel shirt hanging over the top of the door. A couple pairs of well-worn boots decorated the floor beside the wardrobe as well as a pair of dress boots. In the corner of the room there was a washbasin, a large pitcher for water and on one of the corners of the stand was a cowboy hat. The rest of the room reminded her of a motel room. There was a dresser, a nightstand but no mementos anywhere in sight. There were no photographs of family. The bed she was laying in was a brass bed. The four corners were topped with finials. The elaborate designs between the posts didn't really fit with the rest of the room. The bed looked feminine in an otherwise masculine room. The pillows and bedding smelled fresh and clean. The bed had been made this morning. She was lying on top of the covers. The quilts on top of her looked handmade. Smoothing the top of the quilts with her hand, she admired the careful stitching. She glanced over at the window. Snow was blowing around in the wind. She guessed it was cold outside but the window was tight, keeping the cold outside. She heard the wind howl, but it was nothing compared to the fear inside her. She had no idea where she was.

Light shone from the other side of the door that was cracked open. She pushed back the quilt to investigate. Swinging her feet over the side of the bed, she tried to stand. For a brief time she was dizzy. Her legs were weak but after a moment she steadied herself and walked to the door. Peeking out through the crack of the door, she could see a cozy living room. Beyond the living room she saw the kitchen. The roaring fire in the living room offered warmth and lit up the corner of the room. There was a sofa. A rocking chair faced the fire. She could see a small TV in the corner of the room, not turned on. In the silence of the house she could hear someone moving around, but she couldn't tell who it might be. Her stomach growled at the great smells coming from the kitchen, but she tried to ignore her hunger until she knew more about the situation.

Then he came into her line of sight. He was tall and dark haired. Dressed in blue jeans and a red flannel shirt he was cooking something on the stove. She wished he would turn around so she could see his face.

As if he heard her silent request, the man stiffened, slowly turning to face the bedroom door. She backed away for a moment, but didn't take her eyes off the figure in front of her.

His face was lean and long but he had a strong jaw line. He was clean-shaven, tanned from working out in the sun all day long. He had a small cleft in his chin. His eyes, though, held her attention. They were blue.

From where she was she could tell he meant her no harm. His face looked kind but she could be wrong. For a brief second she saw another face in her mind, but before she could remember the face completely it was gone. She took a deep breath and decided to face the man out there. Much as she wanted to, she couldn't stay hidden forever.

Slowly she opened the door limping out of the darkened bedroom. She was still weak so she couldn't move very fast or very far but when he saw her, he rushed to her side to help her to the nearest chair. It was the rocking chair in front of the fireplace. She smiled slightly as she sat down. She couldn't look at him so she kept her face tipped downward.

~ * ~

Colton grabbed an afghan from the couch and spread it out over her legs. When he had touched her arm, her skin still felt cool to the touch. He glanced at her bowed head and frowned. He sat down beside her on the sofa. Staring at the fireplace for a moment, he found he was at a loss as to how to proceed. There were dozens of questions he needed answers for, but she seemed different somehow now that she was awake.

"Who are you? Where am I?" She finally asked. Her voice was low. The voice revealed her state of fear. She hadn't raised her head. Her red hair curtained her face from his gaze.

Colton frowned. He gazed at the woman in front of him as he wondered if she was playing him. This didn't fit with the picture Grayson Trainer had painted. He knew he couldn't trust anything Grayson said—but if this woman had murdered anyone, he would have been surprised. She didn't seem the type, really, given the questions she just asked. "My name is Colton Rivers. I have a ranch about ninety miles from Coven Glade, Minnesota, near a little town called Benton." He watched with interest as she frowned at the information.

"Do you know what happened to me? I mean how did I end up here?" she asked.

"I found your overturned car early this morning. You must have rolled off the road and ended up in the ditch sometime during the night." He shifted his weight to look at her. "Don't you remember the accident at all?"

She shook her head slowly. "Do you know where I was going or where I was coming from?" Her tongue moistened her dry lips. Colton watched, mesmerized by the action. "I'm not sure I even know where this place is."

He blinked twice to clear away the fog then frowned. "What do you remember?"

She turned tearful eyes to him. "I don't remember anything. It's like I woke up for the first time in the bedroom over there. I'm trying, I really am, but I can't remember anything before I woke up."

"Do you know what your name is?" He had to ask. He had been right in thinking her eyes were green. Even with tears in them they were a beautiful green.

She shook her head. The movement must have caused her head to burst into pain. She raised her hand to the wound on her forehead then groaned as she lightly touched the cut on her head. She felt the dried blood as she turned panic filled eyes toward Colton. "What happened to me?"

"You must have hit your head during the accident. When I found you, you were half in, half out of your car. The windshield was cratered; that's what caused the bump on your forehead. I knew I couldn't leave you there. You were cold and wet and, in case you haven't noticed, it is snowing outside. I brought you here early this morning. You were so chilled all I could do was clean the cut on your head and try to warm you up. You've been sleeping almost all day. I checked on you a couple of times."

She glanced at the big picture window, and saw it was getting dark outside. The wind was still blowing the snow around. Crystals of ice were forming on the corners of the window. She shivered.

Colton decided to tell her the police were looking for her. "I had another visitor today. He was mighty interested in finding you."

She glanced at him with curiosity. "Who was he? What did he want?" She was like a child.

Colton grimaced. Her reaction didn't make any sense to him. She should have been more afraid of someone finding her. "It was the local sheriff. The police are looking for you for questioning in a murder case over in Coven Glade." He watched closely for her reaction. "He said you were a dangerous character, you might be armed, and wouldn't hesitate to shoot me in order to avoid getting caught."

She paled. "I murdered someone? Oh my God. . ." her voice trailed off as she thought about that bit of information for a moment. She turned to Colton, "Did the police say who it was I murdered?" She didn't acknowledge the second part of his allegation. It probably didn't make sense to her.

Colton shook his head. "No, all they wanted was information on your whereabouts. Quite frankly, I don't think you murdered anybody." He paused, then remembered something else, "Do you know someone named Ian?"

She frowned then a blinding pain made her close her eyes. Tears welled, rolling down her cheeks. She moaned softly.

"Betty, are you all right." Colton frowned.

She opened her eyes slowly as the pain receded to a dull throbbing pain. She rubbed her temples. Colton saw the pain she was in. "What did you call me?"

"The sheriff that stopped here this morning said your name was Betty Morgan," Colton explained.

She tilted her head. "My name isn't Betty." She frowned. "At least I don't think it is."

Colton sighed. "You never did answer my earlier question. Do you know anyone named Ian?"

She shrugged. "I don't know if I do or not. I wish I could say one way or the other, but I can't even tell you what my name is. I don't know if it's Betty Morgan or something else."

Colton could see how scared she was—how frustrated she appeared to be. He didn't know how to respond so he didn't say anything. He studied her pose for a moment and decided if she was acting she deserved an Oscar. As far as he was concerned she wasn't faking or playing up her situation. She really didn't know who she was or what she was doing here.

He stood up and strode to the kitchen. He put food on a couple of plates then brought them back into the living room where, handing her a plate, he sat down beside her. He started eating.

She stared at the plate on her lap before picking up her fork and eating. She didn't stop eating until her plate was clean. She gazed over at Colton. Surprised, she watched as he grinned. "Sorry, but I was hungry. The food was really great. I don't think I've ever had chicken that tasted so good in my life."

"Don't apologize. You haven't eaten anything all day so you must have been starved." Colton took her plate and his back to the kitchen. He ignored the compliment because he liked to cook, mainly because he had to eat. As a matter of pride, he wanted the food to at least taste good.

When Colton returned he brought two cups of coffee. Handing her one he set the other one on the end table and turned on the television. From the sofa they caught the very end of a news report. It was a grizzly scene as police cars parked in front of a house in Coven Glade. Officers working behind yellow tape took up most of the picture. The house was a simple one. It was painted blue with white trim; the lawn was clipped. There were flowers in bloom in the front border that made it look like whoever lived there took care of the house.

News reporter Shay Phillips stood forward of the yellow tape. He was commenting on the crime that had taken place the night before. "*Police are looking for a woman for questioning in the murder of Ian Carter. Mr. Carter was shot in the house right behind where I'm standing around 2 a.m. this morning. Police are certain a woman they are looking for is responsible for Carter's death. They advise the woman is armed and dangerous. They are asking for your help in finding this woman. She's about five feet two inches tall with dark red hair and green eyes. The police aren't saying at this point what the motive behind the crime is. Please stay tuned for further details.*"

Colton turned the volume down glancing over at her. He was surprised to find her crying while staring at the picture of Ian on the silent screen.

"I guess we know who Ian is now, don't we? We also know the police think I murdered him." Her words were quietly spoken, but they sounded loud in the silence that filled the room. She watched the TV screen, wouldn't look at Colton, staring at the face on the television as if trying to remember who he was. He had a nice face. He was good looking with his blonde hair and soft grey eyes. He was clean-shaven.

"I don't believe the news report." Colton told her. "In fact, I don't think you killed anyone." He snapped the television off. He didn't know what prompted him to say what he felt out loud but once he said the words he found he believed them. She didn't look the type of woman to kill a man, not without a damn good reason.

She turned her head to look at him. "Why? You don't even know me. How do you know I couldn't kill a man? How do you know I'm not the person the police are looking for?"

Colton shrugged. "I'm not really sure why, I just don't think you're a cold blooded killer."

"But the police are looking for me." She sputtered. "You told me yourself a police officer was here this morning looking for me. I'm sure by now everyone in the area is looking for me. You told me yourself the sheriff mentioned I might be armed. I'm considered dangerous! I'll bet every farmer in the area is looking for me."

Colton snorted. "If Grayson Trainer is involved in this investigation, you can bet something isn't kosher. I don't trust him. You know you can't believe everything you hear on the TV. Reporters only report what the police tell them. Grayson said this morning the police wanted you for questioning in a murder, not that you were a suspect in a murder."

She frowned at the name he gave the sheriff that had stopped here this morning. It rang a bell in her confused mind, but she didn't know why. It was the same feeling she'd had when he mentioned Ian's name before they saw the news report. She moistened her lips with her tongue again. "So what happens now? I mean you can't keep me here, you have to call the police and tell them you found me."

"Why?" Colton asked as he sat back on the sofa.

She frowned. "What do you mean, why?"

"There's something about this whole story that doesn't make any sense to me. Until it does I'm not going to turn you over to anyone. "Colton told her simply.

"What about my car? Won't the police find it? If they do, they'll come here looking for me."

Colton shook his head. "The snow will have it buried by morning. If Grayson didn't find it this morning, he won't find it until the snow starts melting. That won't be for at least a day or two. But he could come back here looking for you all the same."

"If he finds me here, you could be in trouble for letting me stay."

Colton grinned. "I'll risk it."

"What about the news report that I'm armed and considered dangerous?" she asked.

"I'm probably more dangerous to you than you are to me right now. After all, you don't know anything about me either," Colton pointed out.

She put her hands around her face, rubbing her temples. She was awfully tired all of a sudden. Her head was throbbing again. "I'm sorry but I think I need to lie down."

Colton nodded. "You can use the bedroom tonight. I'm going to sit here for awhile."

She stood up making her way back to the bedroom. There it was dark and quiet and she needed to be alone. The pillow felt cool to her head. As she closed her eyes she could see Ian's face. Tears welled in her eyes. She couldn't stop herself from crying. Why she was crying she didn't really know, but somehow she thought it had to do with Ian's death.

# Chapter Three

Colton was lying on the couch. He had taken off his shirt and loosened his jeans. A blanket covered his chest. All the lights were off and he was watching the fire burn down. He couldn't help but wonder about his guest and what she had gotten him involved in. How she had gotten from Coven Glade to his back door, he didn't know. He could only guess what really happened in Coven Glade. The house they showed on the news report didn't look like the typical drug house. This house looked like every other suburban house. Like he told her earlier, something about this didn't make sense to him. He needed more information on why the police were looking for her. So many scenarios were running through his head it was giving him a headache. He closed his eyes for a moment.

He awoke a little while later to the rhythmic sounds of the rocking chair. He laid still in the dark not wanting to move until he had a better feel for who was in the house. The glowing embers from the fire told him several hours had passed but still, it wasn't hard to figure out who was sitting in the chair. There was only one other person in the house with him. Then he heard a different sound.

"Are you all right?" He asked her gently so as not to startle her. He had heard her crying in the dark and the sound tore into his heart. He couldn't stand to hear a woman cry.

"No, I don't think so," she told him as she stared into the embers. "Would you like to know what I remembered tonight?"

Colton frowned. "Sure." He had no idea where this was going but he knew whatever she remembered would fill in some of the mystery surrounding her.

"I remembered entering an alley. I think I was following someone but I can't remember why or who I was following. I could hear more than one person talking, but I was too far away to understand what they were saying. I tried to get closer to the voices and I saw two men, one man was holding a gun on another man. They were arguing about something in the box one of them was holding. Then I heard a gun go off and I saw the man with his back to me fall. I remember looking down at him and I saw a red stain on his shirt. I was so shocked I couldn't move. I remembered the man that shot him talking to someone else, but I couldn't see the third man."

"Have you ever seen the man who was killed that night?" Colton asked.

"Yes, he was the man the police said was Ian Carter." Her voice was whispery and low. "But if Ian was murdered in the alley, why would the police say he died in the house we saw on TV last night? I don't understand."

He wanted to tell her to go on, but he also knew the tale was a hard one to tell.

She wiped the tears away from her cheeks and after a few minutes continued with her story. "I was too far away to hear what they were saying. I only caught the tail end of the conversation. They were talking about the box Ian had in his hands. After the man shot him, I knew I couldn't stay there. If they had seen me, they would have murdered me too. When I turned to get away, my foot kicked a bottle across the alley. The killer must have heard the noise because he called out, "Who's there?" I was so scared I took off running. Somebody shot at me but missed. I made it as far as my car, but the killer was right behind me. I knew I had to get out of town so I got in my car and drove. I don't remember driving this far, but I do remember seeing headlights following me the whole way. I sped up to try and lose them, but every corner I drove around they were right behind me.

"The car following me pulled up beside me, and I felt it

bump mine. I almost lost control. I sped up but so did the other driver. He bumped my car again! I felt myself sliding off the road. I couldn't see anything. I hit a tree. My forehead hit the windshield, and I was dazed.

"I remember hearing voices from above me. When I looked up, I saw headlights from another car. I saw the shadow of a man standing at the top of the rise and I felt a moment of panic. I shut off the engine and the lights then waited in the dark for the man to go away. When he finally did, I tried to get out of the car but I must have passed out." She inhaled a shuddering breath.

"Do you remember anything else?" Colton asked. "Wait a minute, you said they. Was there more than one person in that alley?"

"I think there was another man there. I couldn't see anyone else but there must have been someone else." She shook her head. "No, I don't remember anybody else but I have a feeling. It's so confusing; it's like its right there waiting for me to remember."

"What do you mean by that?"

"Have you ever had the answer to a question on the tip of your tongue? It's like I have butterflies floating around inside my stomach, and instead of the feeling going away, it's getting stronger and stronger."

Colton was at a loss as to whether to press her to think until she could remember everything. "I know that feeling." He shivered in the coolness of the room. He stood up to add more wood to the fire.

~ * ~

Her eyes followed him as he moved around the room. For the first time she really studied the man who had saved her life. When he bent over to throw another log on the fire, she saw the muscles in his forearm ripple as he tossed the wood on the glowing embers. His long legs and lean torso looked strong. For a moment she wanted to get up and wrap her arms around him.

Shaking her head she wondered why. When she didn't even know her own name, she was having intimate feelings for a man she didn't know. "I think I'll try and get some rest now. I'm sorry I woke you."

Colton turned and smiled at her. "Hey, no problem. You needed to talk and I'm glad I was here to listen."

She caught her breath at the sight of him when he turned around. His firm, smooth chest was covered in soft dark hair that tapered to his waist. His arms rippled with muscles and his waist was trim. The belt he wore was unbuckled but still in the loops on his pants. He looked so good and she had a feeling she would feel safe in his arms. How she knew she didn't know. She stood up to make her way back to the bedroom.

Closing the door behind her, her eyes caught sight of him again. She felt wanton, warm thoughts, needing his arms around her. This was wrong, she knew, but she couldn't help herself. She pushed the door almost closed but not quite all the way shut.

When she lay down on the bed, the coolness of the sheets was welcome. Her head still hurt. She knew she had to clear her head. The butterflies in her tummy were hard without her understanding what they were trying to tell her. She closed her eyes, drifting into an uneasy sleep.

A while later she began tossing and turning. In her dreams she saw the shadowy man chasing her again, and this time he was getting closer and closer. In her nightmare she was frozen in fear as he closed in on her. Her legs were shaking and she opened her mouth to scream as his shadowy arms grabbed her. Another scent filled her nostrils and it made her sick to her stomach. She could smell the overly-sweet aftershave of the man in the shadows. She still couldn't see his face but she knew he was there and it frightened her. He began shaking her, and she felt his fingers digging in to her arms.

She opened her eyes and he was there. He was shaking her awake. The fear she felt was real. She screamed again and he pulled her closer to him. She tried to pull away from his embrace but his hand held the back of her head against him.

"Hush child, you're safe here. No one is going to hurt you," he kept saying.

She calmed down as she breathed in his scent. It wasn't the sickly sweet scent of her nightmare but instead a clean, musky scent. She opened her eyes to Colton sitting on the bed holding her close to him. "What happened?" she finally asked when she realized she was back in the bedroom. It wasn't a shadowy menace that held her in fear.

Colton released her. She was disheveled and the bed covers were all over the place. Colton smiled slightly. "You must have been having a nightmare. You were calling out to Ian then you were screaming. I tried to wake you up but you fought me all the way."

"Oh my god," she said. "I thought you were the killer." She glanced at Colton. "I was dreaming the killer was closing in on me. I was reliving the scene in the alley. I watched as a man murdered Ian—I knew I was next. Then I was running away from him and he was chasing me. He kept getting closer and closer. I was so scared I couldn't move. That's when he pulled me into his arms. I could smell his aftershave. Then I was struggling with him. I could almost feel the menacing threat to my life. I thought my life was over. When I opened my eyes, all I could see was a man in the shadows and I tried to get away. It wasn't until I could smell you that I realized I was struggling with you."

"I hope you know I wouldn't hurt you," Colton told her.

She nodded. "You've been nothing but kind to me. I know you wouldn't hurt me." She took a deep breath. "I think my name is Bethany Carter. Ian is, err…was my brother. I didn't shoot him, someone else did. I remember the name Nick, and I remember there was a lot of money and drugs involved, but I can't remember why."

"Can we go back to your nightmare a moment?" He frowned as if trying to remember something. "You said the man in the shadows had an over-sweet aftershave. What does that mean exactly?"

Bethany shrugged. "I don't know and that's what's so

frustrating. That night the wind shifted in the alley and for a moment I caught a whiff of aftershave so strong it almost made me sick. I don't know how else to describe it." She glanced at him and said, "You smell clean and fresh and a little bit musky, but the man in the shadows," she could not go on.

Colton didn't know whether to be flattered or feel rejected. "I do wear aftershave you know. I wear Brut."

Bethany shook her head. "Brut blends in with a man's natural scent." She pushed her hair from her eyes. "This aftershave is different. It mixes with the man's scent turning it oversweet and nauseating."

"How do you know so much about men's aftershave?" Colton was curious.

Bethany shrugged. "I guess I'm like most women. I know what I like a man to smell like, and I've always liked the smell of Brut."

~ * ~

Colton sat up. He wasn't sure what any of this meant but it sounded like Ian was involved somehow in the dealing or trading of illegal drugs. "Is that all you can remember?"

She nodded. "Yes, but let me explain a little. Ian was all the family I had left. Our parents died about five years ago in a car crash. They were hit by a drunk driver. I worked at a local restaurant as a hostess, under the name Betty Morgan. That's probably where the name came up."

"Whoa, back up a minute..." Colton was confused. "What do you mean you worked under the name Betty Morgan?"

Bethany turned her head toward him and smiled. "I am an undercover DEA agent, a member of a task force put together in Minneapolis to track the route of a very popular, very new-on-the-market, designer drug called Gentle Breezes."

Colton wasn't shocked. He knew designer drugs were common in the big city, but he also knew they were increasingly more common in rural areas too. The drug trade affected everyone. "And you found those drugs here, in our rural community?"

"We, Ian and I, discovered that Coven Glade was a distribution point. The drugs are brought in from Canada, repackaged then sent out from a warehouse in Coven Glade. We managed to identify at least four couriers and a couple of runners, but we haven't nailed the big boss yet."

Colton leaned back with a thud. "Was Ian a cop as well?"

Bethany touched her wound before answering. "Yes, we were both DEA agents. His undercover assignment was working as a counselor in a group home. He was really making a difference with those kids. I think one of the kids he was working with might be Nick."

"But if you remember all of this why can't you remember the rest of what happened?"

"I don't know. Maybe it has to do with the shooting. I do remember that Ian was shot by a man wearing a blue uniform." Bethany shook her head. "I know I've heard the name Trainer before too, but I can't remember where or when." She looked over at Colton, "You said earlier that you don't trust Grayson Trainer. Why is that? I mean is there a reason you don't trust him or is it that you just don't like him?"

"The whole family is bad. The old man, Seth, is just plain mean. He's treated his wife and kids like dirt most of their lives. When he wasn't smacking them around, he ignored them altogether. Seth is a drinker and when he's drunk, he gets nasty. He has no respect for other people or the law, which is surprising since both of his sons are cops."

"Both of his sons? You mean there's more than one Trainer in law enforcement?" Bethany queried.

Colton nodded. "Grayson is sheriff here but he has a brother Travis over in Coven Glade. Neither one of them is any good. They like to bend the law on the side of illegal almost to the breaking point. Most people around here anyway are afraid of Grayson and what he'll do to them if they don't go along with his point of view."

"And you? Are you afraid of him too?" Bethany wanted to know.

Colton laughed. "I think he's a little bit afraid of me. He knows I don't like him or trust him, but he's left me alone. For now anyway."

"What if he comes back here in the morning?" Bethany asked. "If he finds me here, I have a feeling I won't make it to court. If he or Travis is involved in the local drug activity, they'll shoot first and make up a cover story after the fact."

"That sounds like Grayson and Travis." He thought for a moment before suggesting, "I have a cabin, it's sort of hidden but still on the property I own. We could stay there for a few days, at least until you remember a little more about what happened."

Bethany shook her head. "I can't put you out like that."

"What do you mean, put me out?"

"I can't take you away from your home and what you do," she tried to explain.

"You aren't putting me out. If what you're telling me is going on around here then it needs to be stopped. They need to be stopped. You need to stop them. That's your job. Besides, what happened to your brother? You can't let whoever killed him get away with murder."

Bethany nodded. "I need a safe place to contact my superiors. By now I'm sure they know that Ian is dead and they must suspect the mission may be compromised. I want to catch them both before they have a chance to move in and before the dealers go underground. We'll never catch up with them again if they do that. They'll move to a different town, start up the business. It took eighteen months of surveillance to find Coven Glade."

Colton glanced at his watch. "We have about an hour until daybreak; maybe we should get up and start packing some provisions. I don't think either of us is going to get any more rest tonight."

"Again, I'm sorry I woke you."

"It's okay. I'm glad you remembered more of your past. I

had no clue what Grayson was after yesterday, but if what you said is true, I'm sure he wouldn't hesitate to murder you and call it justified. He already has everyone believing you killed Ian—that you're armed and dangerous. Anyone who sees you would want to call the police and tell them exactly where you are."

Bethany hesitated. "There's something I have to get from my car. Is my car anywhere near this cabin of yours?"

"Yes, we can stop on the way. What do you have to get?"

"I need my gun," she told him.

Colton wasn't sure that was such a good idea. He really didn't know that much about this woman, and now she wanted to retrieve her weapon. He didn't say anything but the thoughts were in the back of his mind. When he glanced at her, he noticed a change had come over her. She wasn't the scared little rabbit she'd been earlier. Had her memory really returned, he wondered, or had she been playing him before?

"We can stop at your car on the way to the cabin to get your gun if you want to," He finally said quietly.

She sighed deeply, "I hear a 'but' in there somewhere. What is it you want to ask me about but don't want to ask out loud?"

Colton raised an eyebrow. She seemed to know exactly what he was thinking, a trait he found very disconcerting.

~ * ~

"Are you worried that I'm lying to get a hold of my gun? That I'll use it to shoot you? Maybe you think everything I've told you about being a cop is a story, and that I might actually be the killer Grayson warned you about?" Bethany guessed correctly. She waited for him to deny it, but when he didn't, it was her turn to raise an eyebrow. "At least you're honest about it." She exhaled and told him. "How about if we compromise? We'll get the gun but you can hang on to it. That way we'll have some protection until you know if you can trust me or not, and I'll have the satisfaction that it's close by. Is that okay?"

Colton grimaced. "That will work for me. Look, it isn't as if I don't want to trust you, but one man is dead, and up until a few minutes ago you claimed not to even know your own name."

Bethany smiled. "I know. Believe me, I would want some kind of reassurance too if I were in the same set of circumstances you find yourself in. After all, I could be lying to you. I'm not, but until you know that for sure I want you to have the advantage."

Bethany stood up and walked to the bedroom door. She didn't have to open it but when she went through it to the living room, she didn't look back at him. Her back had been stiff with disappointment.

~ * ~

Colton glanced through the doorway wondering what he was getting into.

As the sun came up a little while later Colton was in the barn saddling his horse. He thought about taking the truck, but if Grayson did come sneaking around he wanted things as close to normal as possible. Everyone in the area knew he rode his horse around the ranch routinely, plus he didn't want any vehicle tracks leading to the accident at all.

He gazed out into the landscape and was grateful the storm was almost over. Except for the wind that was still blowing, the snow had stopped, and although it was a cloudy day the air had a clean smell to it. He hadn't slept much last night after Bethany told him her story; instead he had gone over every detail. He had still been awake when she started screaming. She seemed honest enough but there was something he felt she was holding back, maybe something she didn't remember yet. Something that might get them both killed.

Colton finished saddling his horse and led it around the back of the house. Tying the reins at the back door he went inside to see if Bethany was ready. She was sitting in front of the television and had the news on. She glanced up when he came in. Colton glanced over at the TV to see what was so interesting.

Grayson Trainer's brother, Officer Travis Trainer, was reporting more of the details of the shooting to the public. "*We believe our person of interest has escaped the city, and we are now canvassing the rural area for the whereabouts of Betty Morgan. She was the last person to see Ian Carter alive. We need to talk to her. If anyone has any information on her whereabouts please call the police at 555-1212.*"

Bethany clicked off the television. Colton frowned as he stared at her bent head. He thought she was crying but he couldn't be sure. "Are you ready to go?"

Bethany wiped the tears away and stood up. She was staring at the blank television screen. Her fists were clenched at her sides. "I'm going to kill that man."

# Chapter Four

Colton glanced at her then looked back at the television screen. "Travis Trainer was the last man I saw on the TV. Why?"

"Because that's the man who shot my brother. He's the one that killed Ian, and he's blaming me for it," Bethany told him. "He was the man Ian was arguing with that night. He was the one that bumped my car off the road."

Colton's eyes narrowed. "Are you sure that he's the one that killed your brother?"

Bethany nodded.

Colton grabbed her by the arms. "I need you to think back to the night your brother died. Was there anyone with Travis Trainer that night?

"What do you mean?"

"You said before "they" were waiting in the alley. Was there someone with Travis that night?"

Bethany thought about that night. She couldn't remember who Nick was or why they were in that part of town. Nor why she had allowed Ian to take the package there in the first place. She had followed him without his knowledge in case there was trouble, but she hadn't stayed close enough to have his back. By the time she'd caught up with him, Travis was aiming his gun at Ian. He had shot him before she could stop him.

"There was someone else there that night, but I didn't get a very good look at him. He was standing in the shadows. You know, I could see his outline in the shadows," Bethany told Colton. "His aftershave stank."

"Come on, we'd better get going," Colton said. "We have a long way to go."

"Why are you so interested in Grayson Trainer?"

"Do you remember what I said earlier about Seth Trainer, his boys, Grayson and Travis?" Colton asked her. When she nodded, he went on to say. "Grayson has always been a bully, even when we were kids he liked to push around the smaller kids. Maybe he felt that way because of how things were at home, I don't know. It sure doesn't matter now. He thinks that because he wears a sheriff's uniform people should automatically respect him. He's mad that I don't. Grayson feels because I don't show him respect then no one else does either. He doesn't realize that it's because of the way he treats everyone that people don't respect him."

"But why did you ask if I saw him that night?" Bethany asked.

"If Travis is into something illegal, then Grayson is right there with him, always two steps behind him. When they were growing up, they had no other friends. Those two boys always did stick together. That's the way it's always been and always will be," Colton told her.

Bethany thought Colton sounded like he had something in mind for the Trainer brothers, but she didn't ask about it. She had her own agenda to worry about. Being this close to Colton wasn't helping her concentration much. She glanced up at him. "Maybe we should go. We can't be here when he comes back. He'll kill both of us."

Colton nodded. "The horse is ready."

Bethany was confused for a moment but she nodded. Colton grabbed a bag off the table and ushered her out to the porch. When she saw the horse standing by the front door, she looked at Colton. She watched him throw the bag over the front of the saddle. When he mounted the horse, she moved to the edge of the step.

Colton held out his hand. She stepped closer to the animal so she could reach out her hand. He hauled her up behind him on the horse.

"I thought we were taking a truck?"

"No," he told her as he reined the horse away from the house. "I don't want to leave any tracks for Grayson to follow. The wind will cover Beau's tracks in no time."

"Well that makes sense. Beau, I take it, is the horse's name?" Bethany muttered as the horse began to move under her.

"Yeah, his name is Beau."

With every step the horse took she could feel his body bump against hers. Her imagination was leading her into dangerous territory.

He steered the horse toward the sound of rushing water. Bethany frowned when she saw the wreck that used to be her car, partially wrapped around a small clump of trees. As Colton had told her, the snow had covered the tracks and had almost covered the entire car. If the trees hadn't stopped her progress down the hill, her car would have come to rest in the creek. Bethany slid off the horse, slipping and sliding over to the car. Brushing snow away she opened the trunk, rummaging around inside for a moment.

She brought out a small black bag. Bethany took a moment to look over her car. *"Maybe if I'd had my gun with me in the front seat or carrying it in the alley instead of leaving it in the trunk of my car, Ian wouldn't have died that night. Maybe I would have found a way to protect him when he confronted Travis."* But she arrived in the alley too late to stop her brother, and just in time to see him executed. She had to live long enough to make sure the man who murdered her brother paid for his crime.

She went back over to Beau and Colton. Colton handed her back up behind him. "Are you ready?"

Bethany nodded saying, "Yes." Colton reined the horse away from the creek toward the tree line. They rode for about twenty minutes before Bethany saw the cabin, small and tucked away where no one would likely know to look. The cabin had a lean-to attached to one side while the front door looked out on the creek. There was a stack of wood inside the lean-to where she could see a couple bales of hay as well. She only hoped that she would be safe until she could get word to her boss.

~ * ~

Colton rode right up to the front door and swung off of Beau then tied him up to the hitching post. He turned to give Bethany a hand off and went to open the front door.

The inside of the cabin was clean and sparsely furnished. Colton wanted to apologize for the accommodations but instead he shook his head. "I'll get a fire going so it will warm up in here."

"It's so cold can see my breath," Bethany said.

Colton loved the cabin. He spent hours here enjoying the peace and quiet. The cabin had a table tucked in one corner, a double bed in the other corner. The two areas were somewhat separated by a sofa placed in front of the fireplace. He tried not to think about the sleeping accommodations. That brought to mind all the wrong ideas. There were other things he needed to think about. He watched her walk to the cupboard and chuckled softly when she opened it.

His gaze was steady as she turned to look at him. Two steps in such a small space brought him to her side where he reached around her and he closed the cupboard again. Then he built a fire in the kitchen stove as well, volunteering nothing.

"What are you doing with a computer and ham radio way out here?" Bethany finally asked.

Colton sighed, a bit of exasperation in that exhalation. He knew he would have to explain things to her. He had hoped to have a little more time to figure this out but time was running short. He nodded for her to sit down at the table. He sat down as well. "I grew up around here, that much of what I told you yesterday is true. I have known the Trainers since we were kids. What I didn't tell you was that when I was eighteen, I moved away from the area. I went to college then after graduation, I joined the Army. I spent the next twelve years with intelligence ops. About three years ago a good friend of mine got into some trouble. I came home to help him."

"Help him with what?"

"He was hooked on Gentle Breezes. He was so messed up there really wasn't much I could do. I managed to get him clean but he was left with a severe personality disorder, and he was never the same again."

"That doesn't explain why you have a computer and ham radio here," Bethany reminded him.

Colton took a deep breath. "Sometimes I come out here to think, to catch up with my old Army buddies. I also do consulting work for the Army. That part's confidential. I have a generator in the lean-to that I can start when I need power. Sometimes I'm here a couple of weeks at a time, but I still need to be able to keep in touch with what's going on at the ranch. My foreman—"

Bethany frowned, "What foreman? I didn't notice anyone else at the ranch."

"He's been at an auction for the last few days. I was out riding line fences yesterday when I found you. Somewhere along the way my ranch work got shoved to the back burner. I'll have to radio Barry when he gets back to the ranch to coordinate a little."

"How big is your ranch, anyway?" Bethany asked. "I haven't seen much of the ranch but I assumed that it wasn't all that big.

"There's a couple hundred acres with about one hundred sixty head of cattle." He shrugged. "It really isn't all that large a spread but the cattle still need to eat. I don't maintain much of the land but I do grow some alfalfa and corn for the cattle."

"Is that what you do? Ranch work I mean. I guess I never asked what you do for a living."

Colton smiled. "I guess that's what I do. I have a pension from the military and some online work, but at heart I guess I'm a rancher."

~ * ~

Grateful the fire was beginning to warm the cabin, she took

off her coat. With a nod toward the cabinet she asked, "Would you let me send a message?"

"Sure, but the reception out here isn't the greatest. It might not go through; even if it does, there's no saying you'll get an answer."

Bethany nodded. "I know but I have to try to make contact. It's already been too long since the shooting. There is a radio frequency I can try to get through on. One only DEA and the FBI use."

Bethany went over to where they had left the items they brought with them. She picked up the black pouch that held her weapon. She thought about keeping it but she knew she couldn't. She turned to Colton handing him the weapon. "I agreed to give you this if you stopped to retrieve it. I want you to know you can trust me."

Colton took the weapon and placed it on the cupboard with the radio in it. He reached around her to grab the bag of provisions before turning his back to her to carry them to the kitchen.

Bethany glanced outside. The wind had picked up as snow kept falling. She knew she was safe, but she was beginning to feel anxious about the lack of contact with her chief. "Did you get Beau put away for the night?"

Colton nodded and disappeared outside for a while. She rummaged about the kitchen, finding sardines, peanut butter, baked beans in cans—enough calories to put a lunch together; although the final result seemed strange, maybe humorous.

By the time she had it finished, Colton came back. He wolfed it down, to her relief, almost without tasting it.

"Well the snow and wind are really raising havoc out there," Colton told her. About mid-afternoon, he had brought in another armload of firewood.

"Great." Bethany was beginning to regret the decision to come out here. Her sense of urgency was growing worse.

"What's wrong?" Colton asked. "I see that look of desperation in your eyes and can hear the impatience in your voice."

"I guess I'm a little jumpy. I'm not used to being so far from civilization. It's kind of creepy." Bethany admitted with a deep sigh, hating to show any weakness.

Colton smiled slightly. "It does seem like we're the only people on earth out here doesn't it. Everything is so quiet. I come out here to clear my mind."

"I can understand why."

The wind had died down for a moment but the snow was still falling. He grasped her hand leading her to the window. "Tell me what you see out there," he asked.

Bethany stared outside. All she could see was snow and trees. "Snow and trees and a whole lot of nothing else."

"Look again, only this time really look," Colton whispered in her ear. He was standing behind her with his hands on her shoulders.

Bethany peered through the window glass. She had grown up in the city; she positively hated the outdoors in the winter. Being cold or wet—those were two things she hated. She frowned as the scene in front of her began to change. It was still snow and trees she saw, but the trees seemed more and more distinct as she observed them, the clearer each tree became. She saw a black squirrel foraging for something to eat in one of the trees. Soon another squirrel ran up to him, and they began to chase each other through the branches. She saw a patch of bright red way up high in another tree. The longer she stared at it the clearer it became. It was a male cardinal; his bright red plumage was beautiful against the dark bark of the tree. Something moved beyond her line of sight. For a moment, she was afraid Grayson had found them, but it was a deer family. The doe moved into the clearing with caution. Behind her came two pretty good sized fawns.

"What do you see now?" Colton asked.

Bethany didn't know how to explain what she was seeing. "I'm beginning to see what I've been missing. It's subtle enough to overlook, unless you take the time to look properly. Everything comes to life if you take the time to see what's really there."

Colton smiled. "Believe it or not, what's out there changes every day; so it's never the same but it's always alive."

Bethany smiled sheepishly. "I guess I never took the time to notice before. I'm from the city so it never occurred to me the country was any different. I guess it was the quiet I never expected. I mean in the city there's always some kind of noise—cars rushing here and there, the sirens of either police or fire truck or ambulances, kids playing right outside your windows, music blasting. It's all plain noise and sometimes it's very easy to block it all out. Out here there is no background noise. Out here my world seems messy and exhausting. The silence is what troubles me and it's what I notice first."

"The isolation can be quite overwhelming at first. The silence alone can drive you crazy if you let it, or it can calm you." Colton told her.

"Can I ask you something?"

"Of course."

"Whatever happened to that friend of yours? The one you helped get clean," Bethany asked.

Colton sighed deeply. "He managed to stay clean. It's taken awhile but he's still clean. He had to hit rock bottom before he could start his life over, but he did it. He found a new job and a new life. He was one of the lucky ones. He told me once that he felt so stupid for getting caught up in something like drugs. He said it never occurred to him that he could get hooked so easily. He became a counselor and now works in Coven Glade. He said he got a second chance thanks to me and his family. He wanted to give others the same chance. He thinks because he went through the same thing they are going through, he can help them adjust to sobriety. He found his purpose in life and making a difference to a lot of people."

"And has he? Helped others reach a state of sobriety, I mean?"

"His program is working. Although lately he said there are some of his people he's concerned about. People like him are getting threats against what they do. Some of the people Scott works with are getting nervous."

Bethany frowned. "Why? What's going on?"

"I'm not sure, but if Coven Glade is a major distribution point and the Trainers are behind the drug trade around the area, maybe the pushers are getting more aggressive."

Bethany sighed thoughtfully, nodding. As much as she wanted to stand by the window watching the day pass, Colton right behind her, she knew it wouldn't bring her any closer to Ian's murderer. And Colton was becoming more important to her than she was comfortable with. "I wish we could get through to my contact. I really need to find out what's going on with the case. I have arrangements to make for Ian."

Colton exhaled sharply, glancing at his watch. "Barry should be back to the ranch by now." He turned her by the shoulders toward the ham radio then sat down at the controls tuning in the frequency. Static crackled. Colton fine-tuned the frequency. He spoke into the microphone; a sprat of garbled talk came back.

Bethany couldn't figure out what was said but Colton made it out.

The conversation lasted a few minutes until the signal became too weak to pick up—the storm interfered with reception. Colton glanced up. "That was Barry. When he got back to the ranch this afternoon, he found Grayson waiting. Grayson had kicked in the back door and searched the house; he left quite a mess. Grayson told Barry he found your car earlier today. He considered it as evidence that I must be hiding you. He told Barry I would be charged with aiding a fugitive if he found you anywhere on my property. He said that Grayson was really pissed and that he made all sorts of threats against me. He also told Barry he would give me twenty-four hours to bring you in. If I didn't, he wouldn't be able to control what might happen."

"Does Trainer know where we are?" Bethany panicked. Grayson must have found the car shortly after they had left it.

"No, Barry didn't tell him a thing." Colton frowned deeply. "Grayson has a lot to answer for. I don't like the fact that he kicked in my door and went through my house without a warrant. I don't care if he was looking for you or not. By threatening me he crossed the line as far as I'm concerned."

Bethany knew in her heart what she had to do. She didn't want to but she knew she couldn't hide forever. "We have to go back," she said quietly.

## Chapter Five

"But you don't have your memory back yet, do you?" Colton asked.

"No, not all of it, but that can't be helped. I won't put you in danger. I can't let Grayson and Travis get away with murder."

Colton drummed his fingers on the table top. "We'll have to wait until morning. I'm not going to risk our lives traveling at night in this weather."

Bethany nodded. At least she would have one more night to remember the rest. She had to remember why Ian had been down in that part of town to begin with. And who was Nick? Where did he fit into the picture, and where was he now? "What about Barry? Will he be all right? Grayson might take his revenge out of him if he can't get to you."

"Barry knows how to take care of himself," Colton told her. "We met while we were in the Army. He was a special ops guy. He isn't afraid of Grayson. If he needs to, he knows how to get into and out of the ranch without being seen by anyone."

"Alright, I don't want anyone else getting hurt because of me. I want to see Ian's murderer brought to justice. I also want to put a stop to drug trafficking in Coven Glen." Bethany glanced at the floor for a moment then turned to look at Colton. "I don't usually talk about this with anyone—I had a girlfriend who was hooked on Gentle Breezes, Faith was her name. We were in high school, but we were best friends since kindergarten. At first she was a recreational user. Then she met Calvin Brooks. Calvin was not a nice guy; in fact I found out he was dealing at the high school. Once he got his hooks into Faith there wasn't anything anyone could do to save her. Believe me I tried. I went to the police but until they could bust him selling drugs, they couldn't touch him. He was a juvenile, so obviously they preferred to work up the chain."

Bethany cleared her throat then went on. "Long story short, one night I found Faith having difficulty breathing with an irregular heart beat. Calvin had sold her a contaminated batch. He walked away from her. She died in the hospital a few hours later. I went looking for Calvin. I found him at the park with another girl.

"I accused him of murdering Faith with his drugs. He laughed in my face and told me she wasn't worth the money to fix her up. She was just another user he screwed when she didn't have cash. I wanted to kill him that night. Lucky for me Ian came looking for me. He'd been worried about me acting out because Faith had died. He had to drag me away from the park.

"Once I calmed down, he swore to me that he would get even with Calvin, but he made me swear I wouldn't go near him again." Bethany felt the tears running down her face as she told Colton her story.

"Did your brother actually stop Calvin?" Colton asked.

Bethany nodded. "Oh yeah, he found a way to stop him. Ian got a bunch of guys together and they all went to talk to Calvin. They convinced him to turn himself in. He went to reform school for a while. After his release, he moved away. As far as I know he's never been back."

"Good Lord, how did they convince him to give up the life, the drug trade, all that money?" Colton asked.

"I have no idea, but there wasn't a mark on him, so they didn't beat it out of him. Calvin would have called on his old buddies if Ian and his friends had laid a hand on him."

"Did Calvin ever accept responsibility for Faith's death?"

Bethany shook her head. "No, he didn't. To him she was just another user prostitute. He knew that once she was hooked, she wouldn't last long. She was lost from the first day. She couldn't save herself, no one could."

Colton nodded. "That's how I felt when my buddy needed me. He lived but he was never the same."

Bethany wiped the tears from her eyes. "Faith was the reason I became a DEA agent; I didn't want anyone else falling through the cracks like Faith. I wanted to make a difference in someone else's life."

"I think you made a difference in Faith's life even if she didn't make it," Colton told her.

Reaching for a Kleenex she went on, "I felt so helpless. I didn't know what to do back then but I do now. The drug syndicate cost me a best friend and now my brother. I know I can't stop it alone, but I can put a dent in it."

Bethany moved over by the window and gazed into the falling snow. She could no longer appreciate the scenery; instead she remembered the night her brother died. How she saw the gun in the moonlight, heard the report as it fired. How he fell. When Travis stepped forward to turn him over, she could see the red stain on his shirt. He was dead.

She knew she had to get out of the alley quickly before they discovered her or they would have killed her as well. Looking back on that night she had remembered the second man, the one who stayed in the shadows. It was he who heard her turn to run. On her way out of the alley, it wasn't Travis's voice but another man's that she heard.

She stood lost in thought until Colton touched her shoulder. She jumped at his touch and abruptly turned to face him. He steadied her as he told her to come to the table for supper.

Bethany glanced from Colton to the window and back to Colton. "Well, I was looking out at the fading afternoon, but now it's dark out."

"You've been at that window for an hour or more. I thought you realized the sun had set."

"I was well and truly lost in thought. I am so sorry."

"So what were you thinking about for so long?" Colton

wanted to know.

"I was trying to think about the night Ian was shot. I was trying to remember something from that night that might help me remember the rest of what happened." Bethany tried to explain. She was increasingly anxious because she knew time was running short.

"Maybe you're concentrating too hard. Let it go for a while, see what happens, "Colton suggested.

"I can't help myself." Bethany cried out. "Travis Trainer shot my brother then he said something to the man in the shadows! I can't for the life of me remember what he said. I need to remember because I—it's important."

"You were probably in shock at seeing Ian gunned down in a dirty alley. Then you were almost caught trying to get away." Colton tried to calm her.

Bethany's eyes searched for a calendar. "What's the date today?" she asked.

"It's December 12th, why?"

"Ian was shot on December 10th. Today is the 12th. I'm sure something is going to happen very soon. The man in the shadows said something about a specific date. Damn, I wish I could remember what he said." Bethany pounded the window sill and turned to face the room, her breathing ragged.

"Hey, slow down. You'll remember." Colton grabbed her shoulders to pull her closer. She tried to get loose of his embrace but somehow she couldn't bring herself to fully break away. In his arms she felt safe from the Trainers. No one but Ian ever made her feel safe before, yet she was afraid of what she was feeling for Colton.

Bethany awkwardly freed herself from his embrace. As much as she wanted to be in his arms, she felt that was too dangerous for her. There was something about the night her brother died she needed to remember. Until then she couldn't possibly know for sure whom she could trust. Colton could be exactly who he said he was, a rancher with no ties to drug trafficking. Or he could be the man in the shadows, the mastermind behind one of the largest drug cartels operating in the United States. She had to remember what she heard that man say.

"I think I'll go to bed. I'm not really hungry. And besides there is really no use us pretending," Bethany told him.

Colton's eyes met hers. He asked, "Pretending what?"

"Never mind, maybe someday I'll tell you, but right now I don't think I can," Bethany said wearily. She walked over to the bed, kicked off her shoes. She lay down and turned her face from him not wanting him to see her tears.

She eventually slept but her nightmare, her ordeal began. She was back in the alley hiding behind a dumpster, trying to make her way closer to where her brother stood facing a man in uniform. She was close enough to hear the exchange between them.

*"So how did you get the package in the first place?" Travis Trainer asked Ian.*

*"It doesn't matter." Ian argued. "I have it. Now I am returning it to you."*

*Travis smiled. "I can see that. What makes you think I know what's in the package?"*

*"The person who gave the package to me told me to return it to you," Ian told him.*

*"And I suppose the person who gave it to you is long gone huh?" Travis nodded as he shifted his position and stepped to his left.*

*Bethany watched with terrified eyes as the shadows behind Travis moved as well. It was too dark to see who or what was there but, definitely, there was movement. Movement in the direction of the pool of light whereby all she saw was the barrel of a gun pointed right at her brother. She tried to scream but she found she couldn't.*

*"Yeah he's gone. I sent him somewhere safe until we get this sorted out." Ian told Travis.*

*Travis grunted. "Until we get what sorted out? That someone has been telling tales out of school? The fact that you brought the package to me in the first place tells me something. But you opened the package as well. In these matters, that's a bad way to do things."*

*Ian nodded. "I had see for myself what was in there."*

*"That's tampering with evidence. How do I know you didn't put drugs in the box? How do I know you aren't an undercover DEA agent making me the target of a sting? How do I know if you're working alone in the area or if you have help?"*

*Travis seemed to know quite a bit about him. Almost as much as he knew about Travis. That's when he saw Travis reaching for the gun on his hip. As if in slow motion Ian turned to run. Travis fired.*

*Travis holstered his weapon. He walked over to where Ian lay. He squatted on his heels, reaching out to turn him over, making sure he was dead. Travis spoke inaudibly.*

*Another voice replied from the shadows. "We have three days until the shipment comes in. We have to find and tie up all the loose ends. We have to find out if Ian was working with anyone else."*

*Travis squinted looking up and into the shadows. "I know what we have to do. We have to find that little bastard Nick to shut his mouth up for good."*

*The man in the shadows leaned forward just far enough that she could barely make out his face. "I will not go to prison for your screw up. Fix this! Fix it now." He backed away talking to someone else but she couldn't hear what he said.*

Bethany sat up in bed and screamed. She felt strong arms about her. Someone whispered that everything would be all right. Bethany was crying, sobbing Ian's name over and over.

# Chapter Six

Colton held her until she stopped crying. He'd been asleep on the sofa when the nightmare began. Her restless tossing and turning awakened him. She had talked through the entire event reliving her helpless role as witness to the murder of her brother.

Bethany finally calmed down enough to see by the faint light of the fire the single room the sofa and table of the cabin so far from roads that she knew herself to be safe. Colton's arms were around her. She pushed herself away a little to be able to see Colton's face. She saw genuine concern there and something else.

"What did you overhear?" she finally asked.

"Everything you saw happen the night your brother died," he told her. "Was Nick the person who gave your brother the package?"

Bethany nodded. "Ian was working with him. He's one of the kids from the center. "

"Do you know where he is now?"

Bethany shrugged her shoulders, seeming to release a knot of tension. "I think so."

"Who is the man in the shadows?" Colton asked.

Bethany dropped her head. "I don't remember if I ever saw his face clearly. He leaned forward into the light under the streetlamp to talk to Travis but his face was still shadowed, and I was too far away. He's the guy who wears the nauseating aftershave."

She hadn't been able to add anything to her earlier recollection of last night. He focused on her face." Are you alright?"

"So much has happened in the last few days. I haven't been able to get enough sleep to make a difference."

"Ok, I'll be on the couch if you need anything." As he moved to rise and leave the bed, his arms moving to his side, colder air found her as the space between them widened.

Bethany panicked. "Please can you stay here with me? I don't know if I can handle being alone right now."

~ * ~

Colton hesitated. He lay down on the bed and pulled her back into his arms. Something stirred inside him and as much as he tried to quash what was happening, he knew the effort was futile. At least, he hoped, she wouldn't notice what was happening.

Bethany nestled her head on his shoulder. He was amazed at the heat radiating from her body. He heard the steady beat of her heart as it pounded in her chest. He breathed in her natural scent.

Colton felt a change come over her. She felt right in his arms and he wondered what it meant. He closed his eyes and he too drifted to sleep.

Some time later Colton was roused by a noise. At first it was too faint to detect but the longer he heard it the louder and more annoying the noise became. It grew closer then it faded again and again. Colton propped himself up in bed on one elbow. He listened for the annoying sound. It reminded him of the buzz of a dragonfly in the summer time, but it wasn't summertime now.

He shook Bethany, "Do you hear that? Listen."

Bethany cocked her head and listened. At first she didn't hear anything but then she too heard the buzzing. She glanced at Colton. "That sounds like a snowmobile."

"Damn!"

"Do you think it's could be Grayson looking for us?" Bethany asked.

"It might be." Colton agreed. "He knows I'm not at the ranch. He'd figure I couldn't be very far away. If he checked, he would find my truck in the barn, and he knows I ride horses when I'm home." Colton stood up and walked over to the windows. "Trainer might not know about this cabin, but it won't take him long to find it. They'll spot it as soon as the sun comes up."

Bethany sat up in bed. "What can we do?"

Colton glanced over at her from the windows. "We'll have to keep watch. If they come too close, we'll have to be able to move at a moment's notice."

"How are we going to do that?" Bethany asked.

"We'll have to go on Beau. He's the only transportation we have at the moment," Colton told her. "On a horse we can go places a snowmobile can't."

Bethany stood up and joined him at the windows. "What have you got in mind?"

Colton walked over to the cabinet and handed the black pouch to her." You keep watch while I go saddle Beau. That way we can get out before they get here if we see them coming. If they don't find us before dawn, we'll start out as soon as the sun comes up."

Bethany took her weapon out of the pouch, loading it before Colton walked outside to saddle his horse. No light shone inside the cabin to give away their position or turn the glass in the window into a mirror. She was surrounded by darkness.

Each time he caught the whine of the snowmobiles his heart sped, but the lights he saw in the distance never shown toward the cabin.

Colton finished saddling Beau and came back to help her keep watch.

All too soon the sun was above the horizon, Colton wanted to go back in time and dig a little deeper into Bethany's memories of the murder. In that brief unguarded moment he remembered that flash of desire and something else. He glanced over at Bethany. She was looking back at him, her eyes guarded, and so the moment was lost.

Colton could see the storm had completely blown over and the sky was clear. He didn't know what the day would bring, but he knew they couldn't wait any longer to get away from the cabin. He opened the cupboard that housed the ham radio to call his foreman, Barry. He needed to know what was waiting for them at home. The broadcast was brief, and when he signed off Colton glanced over at Bethany. He said, "Everything is quiet at the ranch but Barry doesn't trust it will stay that way."

"What does that mean? He doesn't trust what?"

"He knows the Trainers are close by. He's found tracks near the cattle pens, but nothing is out of place. He saw snowmobile tracks all over the fresh snow on his way in this morning. He said he can almost feel their eyes watching his every move." Colton stood up and grabbed his jacket. "We should get out of here now before the snowmobiles circle back."

~ * ~

Bethany looked around the cabin. She was going to miss it. She didn't know why, she had never been one for the outdoors scene, but she knew she was going to miss the hush as night fell, the warmth of the stove, the physical nearness of Colton. She stood and walked to the big window. She saw the clear sky and the fresh layer of snow. She was glad the storm was finally past.

Colton caught her eye as he closed the door to the cabinet. He seemed upset.

"What's bothering you?" Bethany asked.

"I told Barry to go home to stay until he hears from me. I don't want him caught in the crossfire. Damn it." He swore as he shrugged into his jacket. "They must want you really bad. Grayson wouldn't be this bold otherwise."

"That's not good." Bethany thought out loud.

"What else did you see that night?"

Bethany pressed her hands to her head, obviously searching

for the smallest item. "I've told you everything I can remember."

"There has to be something else." Colton began to pace. "Grayson wouldn't push this hard if there weren't something more damning."

Bethany shrugged. "I honestly can't remember anything else. I never saw the face of the man in the shadows and I can't remember what he told Travis before I ran."

"There has to be something more." Colton placed a heavy hand on her left shoulder, giving it a shake. "You have to think. Can you remember anything else from that night?"

"No I can't." Bethany struggled from his grasp. "Don't you think I would have told you already if there were? I don't know why Grayson wants me dead. Or what happened after they shot my brother. I just don't know."

"I'm sorry." Colton ran his hand through his hair. "You must know this is hard on me as well as you."

She rubbed her upper arms trying to keep a shiver from snaking up her spine, "What's the nearest town around here? I really need to make a phone call."

"There's a phone at the Four Corners. That's a bar at the corners where I-90 crosses Interstate 61. It's not that far from here," he told her.

Bethany nodded. "Good, let's go then. The sooner we start the sooner this will be over."

Colton made sure the fire from the night before was out and a few minutes later they were on their way. Colton steered his horse away from the cabin. They had to go through the trees and when they came out the other side, Bethany could see the highway and the bar in the distance. They were about to break out of the tree line when Colton backed his horse up. Bethany peeked over his shoulder to see what the holdup was and that's when she saw the parade of police cars coming down the road.

Four police cruisers, all with their red and blue lights flashing came right at them. It wasn't until the cars passed where they were that Bethany exhaled the breath she was holding. Turning her head she watched as the four police cars split up at the off ramp. Two went left and the other two went right. The two cars that went left took the off ramp to the interstate road and the two cars that went right were going toward the small town of Benton.

"I wonder whether that parade has anything to do with us." Bethany said.

"You can bet Grayson won't like the extra cops around," Colton murmured.

"What do you mean?" Bethany frowned.

"Grayson and Travis are out at my place with a crew you can bet aren't police officers. They'll have the few men who don't mind breaking the law for the Trainer family. They can get away with a lot if Grayson and Travis are in charge. They can get away with murder."

"That doesn't sound good," Bethany whispered. "The sooner we get to a phone the better. The bureau can take you into protective custody until this is over."

Colton was instantly dismissive. "I go to jail while Grayson and Travis break the law. Somehow that doesn't sound right."

"It wouldn't be for long and you won't go to jail. You'll be going to a safe house until we have everything we need to put them away for life."

"I still don't like it." Colton murmured as he moved his horse toward the road.

# Chapter Seven

As Bethany approached the restaurant the more intensely she felt that the events of the past few days would dominate her actions, to the point of distracting her from the objective of this mission. Making contact with her chief had to be paramount. The next few moments were all she had to collect and sort the newest developments in the case against the drug Lords. Her only time, now, to learn what others might know about the death of her brother.

When they crossed the road and reached the payphone, she felt more than saw Colton dismount the horse. Bethany turned, lifting her right leg over Beau's rump and slid off the horse right into Colton's arms. As much as she wanted to stay right there and let the rest of the world go by, she pushed herself away. Inside the phone booth, she dialed the operator, asked for a collect call, and gave the number.

A few minutes later she returned to Colton. "Well, that's done."

"What exactly is done?" Colton asked.

"Within the hour the DEA will raid the warehouse and arrest everyone inside. There are agents on the way to your ranch to arrest the Trainer brothers and anyone else who happens to be at the ranch. If they find drugs at the warehouse, that will close the case. At any rate Travis Trainer will go to jail for the death of my brother," Bethany told him.

"What about Grayson Trainer?" Colton asked.

Bethany shook her head. "I told them I couldn't see the man in the shadows. If Grayson is involved, we'll have to find the evidence to connect him to the crime and to his brother."

"What are we supposed to do?" Colton wanted to know.

"We are supposed to wait here. Someone will pick us up after the arrests are made." Bethany looked around. She didn't really want to spend the morning in a bar but then she noticed there was a restaurant too. "Let's go get some breakfast. I'm starved."

~ * ~

Colton nodded and tied the horse up. Inside they chose a table. Neither of them said too much while they ordered and ate. After the meal was over, though, Bethany kept a close eye on the front door. Colton knew she was waiting for someone to come and pick her up. It seemed to him she couldn't wait to go back to her life in the city.

When the door finally opened and a stranger walked in, Bethany smiled and waved at him. Colton knew the time had come to say goodbye. Unresolved feelings flooded his body as he realized he might never see her again. When they stood up he reached for her and pulled her into his arms. He bent his head and kissed her with all the passion he felt for her. Then he let her go.

Bethany looked stunned. He hadn't been looking forward to saying goodbye and his kiss had weakened his defenses, not to mention it had taken his breath away. The feelings he had been trying to hide all along had come out in his response. The look in her eyes had told him that she understood.

The stranger joined them before either could say another word. Bethany had to clear her throat to greet him, "Hey, Ron, how did it go?"

Ron smiled. He looked from her to Colton and back. Red in the face but smiling at the corners of his mouth, he made his report. "We got it all. The raid on the warehouse was barely in time. They were already loading the stuff on several trucks headed for places unknown, but we managed to stop them before any of the trucks drove out the door."

"Was there any gun play?" Bethany asked.

Ron nodded. "There was some resistance but we managed to get the drop on them. It was over before they had a chance to really get into a firefight."

Bethany smiled. "I've always known I can't halt the flow of drugs, but anytime I can put a hole in the pipeline is a great day, and so worth the effort. What about the guys out at Colton's ranch? Did you manage to get the Trainer brothers into custody?"

Ron smiled. "Oh yeah, but we only got one of them. He tried really hard to convince us he was on our side of the law but it didn't work. After the raid on the warehouse, several of the guys we busted spilled their guts about the guys in charge. They were looking for a deal before we even cuffed them."

"Which one did you get?" Colton asked.

"We got Travis. Apparently Grayson bolted when he saw the DEA and FBI moving in." Ron continued, "He and three other people got away. We chased them but they all separated and as we didn't have snowmobiles, we just watched them go. Until we catch up with him, you both need to go under wraps."

Bethany glanced over at Colton. "I know you won't like hiding—" she began

No, and he didn't want to leave her quite yet. They had to talk about that kiss.

Bethany nodded. "By the way, Travis is the one that murdered Ian. I saw him shoot my unarmed brother in cold blood."

Ron sobered for a moment. "I'm sorry Ian is gone. He was a nice guy. We've taken care of his body. He's at the morgue waiting for you to decide how you want to care for his remains."

Colton saw the tears burning in her eyes and his heart wrenched for her.

"Well, it looks like you're still stuck with me for a little longer. It shouldn't take too long to run Grayson down. Then you can have your life back."

"What about Beau? I can't leave my horse here alone."

"Can you call Barry and have him take Beau back to the stables?" Bethany asked.

"I suppose that would work best, although I hate leaving him her."

"We can get someone to stay with him until Barry gets here with the trailer," Ron offered. "But we need to get the two of you somewhere safe, fast."

"Ok, let me call Barry to make arrangements for Beau and then I'll go with you."

Bethany watched him walk outside and pull out his cell. She turned to Ron and asked, "What happened at the ranch?"

Ron frowned. "We came in on two sides. There was a firefight. We saw part of the group bolt. Three of the men escaped. We managed to get the remainder of the group contained and the FBI went after the three who got away. They found snowmobile tracks behind the ranch. That's where they split up and disappeared into the woods."

"Damn," Bethany swore.

The door opened and a man with a gun strode into the restaurant. Ron saw him come in too—he pushed her to the floor. He reached for his gun but the intruder raised his weapon and got a round off. Ron went down clutching his shoulder.

From outside Colton watched Bethany fumble for Ron's gun then begin firing at the man by the door. Her first bullet hit him in the chest and knocked him off his feet but it didn't put him down. The man shot off another round. His bullet splintered the table over her head. Her second bullet put a hole in the man's forehead. The gunman dropped to the floor. Everything happened so fast Colton hadn't had time to even think, he simply watched her react, a blessed consequence of endless training. Feeling sick to his stomach, he went to get Beau.

~ * ~

Ron was struggling to sit up, holding his shoulder, in pain and rapidly going into shock, but he was alive. Bethany looked at the front door. She hadn't seen Colton come back in before the bullets flew. She glanced back at Ron and found the bartender holding a cloth to Ron's shoulder. She knew he would be taken care of. "I'm going to find Colton. I didn't hear any shooting outside but he might be hurt."

Ron nodded. "Be careful out there. There are two more suspects at large."

She nodded, scrambled to her feet, and went for the door. She still had Ron's gun in her hand, automatically checking the load as she carefully scanned the lot around the door. There was no sign of Colton or his horse. She opened the door part way and slowly slid through it, plastering herself against the wall of the restaurant. She couldn't see anyone but if the man she shot was one of Grayson's men, she couldn't take the chance that Grayson wasn't out there somewhere.

Bethany turned back into the restaurant. Going out the back door she made her way around the building. She found Colton's horse but again there was no sign of Colton. She turned to go around the other way and ran into a man's arms. "Colton! Oh thank god. I was looking for you."

"I had to get some fresh air. How is Ron?" Colton asked quietly.

"A man walked in and started shooting. Ron will be fine," Bethany told him. "I've never seen him before."

"I have. He's one of Grayson's men, Jared Fry," Colton admitted. "I saw him from the corner of my eye when I brought Beau around the side of the bar."

"Did you see Grayson out there somewhere?" Bethany asked.

"No, Grayson wouldn't be here." He pointed toward the other side of the road to the snowmobile sitting there. "You can be sure he sent Fry. I was about to come in behind him when the shooting started so I stayed out of sight."

"So where is Grayson, do you think?"

Colton rubbed his chin with the back of his hand. "Hiding. I'll have to think about where he might go. Jared must have found our tracks by the cabin and followed them."

"Either that or Grayson is smart enough to have had someone waiting for us at the nearest phone in the area. The quicker we can get to the safe house the more time the agency men will have to find him. Bethany took his elbow. "Let's go see how Ron is. Jared shot him in the shoulder."

Colton followed her back inside the restaurant. Ron was sitting in a chair while one of the staff manufactured a pressure bandage from several laundered kitchen towels. He badly needed to see a doctor.

Ron glanced up at Bethany. "I called the DEA office. They are sending another team to pick you up." He gazed over at the dead man. "Do you know who he was?"

Colton nodded. "Jared Fry. He's one of Grayson's men."

"Three men escaped the ranch this morning. He could have been one of them," Ron told them. "Grayson is still out there somewhere."

A few minutes later two agents entered the restaurant, Steve Houser and Ben Loock. They quickly assessed the situation. "We have orders to take Bethany and Colton Rivers into custody and you to the hospital."

"Have you heard anything new about Grayson Trainer yet?" Ron asked as he got to his feet.

Steve shook his head. "No, but we have all possible police personnel looking for him." Steve glanced back at the front door to the body on the floor. "We'll call an ambulance for that one."

Ron nodded. "Bethany shot him before he could finish what he started."

Ben looked over at Colton. "I'm ready to take you and Bethany to a safe house. Steve will stay here with Fry until the ambulance gets here then he'll meet us."

"Barry will be here in about ten minutes to take Beau home. I told him I'd check with him in a few days. It shouldn't take much longer than that for you to bring in Grayson."

A few minutes later the ambulance pulled up. The medics argued hard to take Ron with them as his situation had deteriorated. Ron kind of minded riding with a corpse, but in the end he had no choice. Ben drove Colton and Bethany about forty miles to a town called Winona. Turning off highway 61 onto Huff Street Ben drove through town toward the Mississippi River. Ben took Huff Street right into the heart of the city. He turned on Broadway and traveled several blocks to Walnut Street. Turning left he traveled several more blocks before he pulled into a driveway on the left, a light blue house on the corner of the block. The safe house faced the Mississippi River. They could see ice along the shoreline from where they stood.

Bethany, Colton, and Ben got out of the car walked to the front door. Bethany glanced down the street but didn't see anything out of order. All the other houses in the area were a little run down. They wore fading and peeling paint while their sidewalks hadn't been shoveled since the last snowstorm. Yet everywhere she looked she could see signs of the Christmas holiday. The porch across the street had Christmas lights wrapped around the railing, a Christmas tree in the window. The red and green lights sparkled through the glass. The neighborhood looked quiet, homes sat on large lots making rows of just five to a block face. It was just the place to hide in plain sight. Ben dug in his pocket and pulled out a ring of keys. He unlocked the front door and inside they all went. Ben let Steve know they had arrived safely then went out to scout the perimeter.

~ * ~

Colton sat down on the sofa and watched them at work. In the first place, he wasn't happy being there. He'd rather have been able to go back to his ranch. He had been unusually quiet throughout the trip down here, and he didn't have too much to say right now. He had been thinking about where Grayson Trainer might hide out. Likewise, he had been thinking about the kiss he gave Bethany. Starting out of a brown study, he looked in her direction only to find her looking back at him. When she winked at him, he was surprised and intrigued. "Where are we exactly?" Not much of a conversational starter, but the best he could do at the moment.

"We're in Winona. It's a small town on the Mississippi River," Bethany told him.

"I know where Winona is. In case you've forgotten, I live in Minnesota," Colton told her gruffly.

Bethany closed her eyes. "I didn't mean to patronize you. I forgot you grew up here. I guess I've forgotten quite a lot the last few days."

"But you started to remember things, too." Colton reminded her.

Bethany nodded as she looked around the room. "I have started to remember but Ian is still dead, and you and I are hiding out until Grayson Trainer is in custody."

Ben joined them and said, "The word is Ron is going to be fine. He's on his way back to Minneapolis. We're supposed to stay here tonight and check in with Steve tomorrow. They found the other men who got away with Grayson but they haven't found Grayson yet," Ben told them.

Bethany nodded but asked Colton, "Do you have any idea where Grayson would go if he were hiding?"

Colton shook his head. "He knows the woods pretty well, although if he were really in trouble, he might go back home. Seth Trainer is a mean bastard, but he wouldn't allow his sons to come to any harm. He doesn't much care for any unrelated members of law enforcement."

Bethany stretched and covered a yawn. "They just play cops. They don't really enforce any laws."

Colton's mouth twisted in what passed for a grin. "Seth figured he could work with them to monopolize local law departments." Colton sat back on the sofa. "They used fear and intimidation and kept their noses clean, at least on the surface. They know enough about forensics to clean up a crime scene before anyone else gets there. They never would leave enough evidence to condemn themselves." He paused and shook his head. "Until now."

"Until now? What are you thinking?" Bethany asked.

"Now Travis is behind bars while Grayson is on the run. A Trainer behaves, when threatened, like a wounded animal. If you back one of them into a corner, he will fight for his life, so more people are going to get hurt."

Bethany looked closely at his expression. "What are you saying?"

"I'm saying that Grayson won't come quietly once you do find him. If he figures he's caught, there is going to be a gunfight. He isn't going to be happy that Travis is sitting in jail."

"Ok, how can we get to him with minimal damage control?" Ben asked.

Colton shrugged. "I think we are going to have to convince him that Travis is going to talk. Grayson will see today as a failure. Reason number one: Travis got busted so his brother is in jail even though he's not. Reason number two: he'll think I probably set him up so he's going to link me with ending his career. He'll more than likely come after me because he can and he still has to get Bethany. But she's not the only witness who can place him at Ian's murder. Right now the charges against Grayson aren't that serious. They are circumstantial, but if the state police convince Travis that Bethany's testimony and his would give him room to bargain for a reduced sentence in exchange for catching Grayson, we stand a better chance of finding him before he surprises me and Bethany."

Ben nodded. "Ok, say all of this is true, how do we stop him?"

Colton shook his head. "You aren't going to like my idea."

"If it involves using yourself as a target, forget it," Bethany told him. "I see where the conversation is going and I don't like it."

Colton switched his gaze to her for a moment then turned to

look at Ben. "It might be the fastest way to catch him, if not the only way to catch him."

Ben had certainly read the look that passed between the two and didn't quite know what to think. He didn't want to get in the middle. "I'll have to talk this over with my supervisors, but it might be the only way, like you said."

Bethany growled. "You can't, I won't allow it. He'll kill you without even thinking about it. He hates you and all you represent."

Colton glanced at her and smiled. "I won't let that happen. Don't you know that the good guys always win?"

"Not always they don't. Sometimes the good guys die young," Bethany reminded him with tears in her eyes. "My brother was a one of the good guys."

"Not this time. I won't let him kill me."

Bethany could read the expression in his eyes and knew there was nothing she could say to change his mind. She was afraid for him but she was also afraid for herself. She didn't understand her feelings for him and that confused her. She had always been so sure of herself in the past.

## Chapter Eight

The evening passed slowly as they waited for word from the boss in Minneapolis. If they agreed to Colton's plan, they would go back to the ranch to wait for Grayson come to them. Bethany couldn't look at Colton let alone talk to him. She didn't want to put his life in danger, yet she knew it might be the only way to get to Grayson.

Ben called for pizza. As they ate supper there was very little conversation.

Bethany took first watch in order to let Ben sleep. There was no activity at that hour while the time alone would give her time to think. She needed it. She was glad Colton had disappeared behind the door of the bedroom. She sat on the couch thinking about everything that had happened over the last few days. The longer she thought the more confused she became. Finally, she glanced over at the bedroom door Colton had gone through.

She got up off the couch and marched over to the door. She reached for the knob and turned it before she had time to stop herself. The moonlight coming through the window shown on his sleeping form. He lay there with the covers up to his waist. His chest was bare; she could see that soft mat of hair rise and fall with his every breath.

Bethany licked her dry lips. She couldn't take her eyes off him. It would be very easy for her to join him, just let things happen. She wanted him—she thought he wanted her if their first kiss was anything to go by. *Would it be so bad?*

But instead of joining him in bed, she walked over to the window, glancing out at the city beyond the glass. It was a quiet town, but to her it was just another town. She could see the river below, it looked cold and menacing. Christmas lights gave the town a festive air but the streets were quiet. As she gazed she couldn't help but wonder if nights in strange houses would be her life. She had no ties, here or anywhere, now that Ian was gone. Winona didn't matter.

She was so lost in her own thoughts she didn't hear Colton until she felt his arms come around her, cradling her body. "And how is the city tonight? Are there any demons or other bad guys out there coming for me?"

Bethany sank deep within his arms, marveling at the sensations. Conflicted, she thought never had anyone else made her feel so sheltered. From the first moment, she had had nothing to fear from him. "I don't know about out there."

She felt Colton's sighs stir her hair. "What about in here?"

Bethany blushed. "That would be me, wouldn't it?"

"And what would you be interested in?" she heard him chuckle in her ear.

"That's a very good question, isn't it?" she whispered." One I don't have an answer for."

He turned her around to face him. As Bethany's arms went around him she felt his bare skin. "Maybe this will help," Colton whispered as his lips met hers.

Bethany opened her heart and her mind as sensation after sensation ripped through her. Her heart pounded in her chest as she felt her blood quicken in her veins. Her body melted into his, her hands ran up and down his back. Bethany barely noticed the lack of clothing as her hands roamed down his back to his hips and beyond.

Colton inhaled deeply when her hands slipped around the front of his body. He picked her up and carried her to the bed. Laying her down carefully, he followed her down to the comfort of the waiting haven. As his lips found the pulse on the side of her neck, he heard Bethany groan with pleasure. His fingers found the buttons of her shirt. In seconds she was flesh to flesh with him.

Bethany paused for a moment to look into his eyes, eyes that held the promise of things to come. Her body cried out for the release only he could give her. She reached her hand to touch his face. She could tell he wanted her. Lord help her she wanted him. She reached for his lips and let loose the last barrier between them.

Colton surged ahead and slipped inside her. Bethany was ready. Soon their world exploded as they climbed higher and higher. Every stroke lifted them up as the heat from their coupling grew.

Bethany groaned as his lips found her nipples. As his tongue lathered her ripe breast, what she was feeling almost sent her over the edge. She pulled his head to her. As her lips met his she exploded into mindless passion.

Colton felt her slip over the edge, and he, with one final surge, joined her in paradise. "Beth," he cried out as he slumped on top of her and moved to her side. Bethany felt happily spent. She had glimpsed paradise in his arms and didn't care if she never left them.

Colton cradled her close to him and closed his eyes. His heart was still pounding in his chest. He had just tasted her passion. For just a moment, he forgot about the rest of the world. Nothing mattered more to him than sharing this moment with her.

"Wow," Bethany whispered as she turned to kiss him. When their lips met, they both felt the sizzle.

Colton deepened the kiss, wanting more. He slid his leg around her waist. Bethany turned into the kiss. She felt her heart miss a beat. When Colton's lips moved down to her throat she tried to break the assault on her senses.

"Please wait," she begged. Her breath was ragged and her voice was little more than a whisper.

Colton groaned, pulling away. He rested his head next to hers and waited for his heart to slow. He glanced over at her and his heart broke at the look in her eyes.

"I'm sorry," she whispered.

Colton closed his eyes. "Please don't be sorry. I would be

devastated if you were sorry."

Bethany cupped the side of his face. When he opened his eyes, she smiled. "I'm not sorry we made love. That was wonderful."

"But? I hear a but coming," Colton replied.

Bethany glanced at him. "I'm not sorry we made love but the timing could have been better," she finally told him. "We still have Grayson and Travis to deal with. We don't know the outcome to that situation yet."

"I understand all of that but I think the timing was perfect," Colton told her.

"You may be right but I have to take a step back to see what happens tomorrow."

Colton wanted to protest but his heart stopped him. "Okay we'll wait."

Bethany heard something in his voice that told her he couldn't wait long. Whatever happened tomorrow would make or break their time together.

Bethany parted from him and picked up her clothes. She dressed in silence. At the door she looked back where she saw Colton, his arm draped over his eyes. Closing the door quietly behind her, she knew she was closing him out. Crossing the room to the sofa, she sat down.

Lost in thought, she missed Ben's door opening. When he saw her sitting there with tears on her face, being the wise man he was, he stepped back into his room, silently closing the door. When the sun came up the next morning, Bethany hadn't slept at all—she was much too wired to feel sleepy. Colton's face was a closed book. Ben obviously pitied her. "I heard from Steve. He said he would be in place at Colton's ranch by ten this morning," Ben told them.

Bethany glanced at her watch. "That's about the time we'll get there if we leave within the next hour."

"He also told me that Travis Trainer was bailed out of jail before the new charges could be entered," Ben told them quietly.

Bethany quickly glanced at Colton then she looked to Ben.

"How could that happen?"

Ben shrugged his shoulders. "Judges have a hard time keeping a cop in jail. Now we have two men on the loose with nothing to loose."

"Don't forget their father," Colton said softly. "Seth will fight right along beside them."

"We have to be in place when they get there," Bethany said.

"Let's go then. I want this to be over," Colton agreed.

No one said a word during the trip to Colton's ranch. The closer they got to the ranch the more anxious Bethany became. The more anxious she became the more she retreated into her professional, armored self.

# Chapter Nine

When Ben turned into Colton's driveway everything looked to be untouched, in place. Ben pulled up to the house where he let Colton out of the car to go into the house. Bethany and Ben followed him. Inside Bethany watched Colton choose a rifle from his gun cabinet, check the action, and load it. The smallest sounds echoed in the silence of the house.

Their eyes met across the room but neither said a word. Bethany had to glance away. From the side windows she began scanning the area. She wasn't looking for signs of wildlife this time.

Bethany closed her eyes just for a moment. She searched through the backyard going from tree to tree, bush to bush. Then she changed windows, scanning the side yard. As the sun moved closer to the middle of the sky, the shadows changed. She saw something move behind the shed.

Bethany motioned Ben to her side. Silently she pointed toward the shed; she whispered at him, "I saw a shadow move on the back end of the shed."

Ben watched for a moment or two then he nodded.

Bethany whispered, "I'm going to check the back yard again."

Ben said, "Colton is watching the front. I received a text from Steve. His men are moving in from the woods. If the Trainers are out there, hopefully we'll catch them before they get close enough to the house."

"Hopefully before they kill someone." A shot rang out.

Bethany ducked. The window frame beside where she was standing exploded. Another shot rang out from behind the shed and Bethany leapt back. Ben slid into her place. He fired a couple rounds in the direction of the shed.

Colton struck the glass of the east-facing window with the butt of his rifle. The breaking glass fell to the floor. Colton raised his rifle to a firing position, immediately snapping off a few rounds.

Bethany, listening intently between shots, heard foot steps upstairs. She moved to a spot behind the staircase, waiting with her weapon ready to fire. A few more steps. A pause. She peeked around the corner of the staircase. A pair of boots was coming down. A second passed, then another. The boots became a pair of legs.

She stepped out from her hiding place, her gun on the kneecaps of the pair of legs. One more step. The face of the man appeared—a small man with a weapon in his hand. He clearly saw her as he lifted the gun. She saw his finger tightening on the trigger.

Bethany didn't give him a chance to fire. She shot him point blank. He fell forward and across the stairs, through the banister and hit the floor beside her.

Bethany stepped over him and back to the bedroom window. In the backyard, shapes moved from one shelter to another. She waited, watching for a moment as the shadows move in closer to the house. Cracking open the window sash, she took aim across the windowsill. The shadow moved again and she saw Travis Trainer's face come into view.

Bethany squeezed the trigger on her gun. Her aim was high. It shattered the branch above his head. A splinter of wood pierced his face and Travis screamed in fury. He ducked back behind a tree, aiming in her general direction.

All hell broke out as gunshots from all sides peppered the house. There were shouts, more gunshots. Bethany had to duck when Travis fired a shot her way. She didn't think he knew where the bullet that hit the branch came from. Bethany took aim again. This time her shot hit its mark. Travis took the bullet in the shoulder. He hit the ground hard, rocking back and forth as his gun landed three feet away from him.

Bethany climbed through the window. She ran up to him with her gun trained on him, ignoring the possibility that another of the shadow team might see her. With her foot she kicked the gun farther away from him.

"You bitch, you shot me," Travis growled as he writhed in pain. He grimaced in agony as one hand squeezed his shoulder.

"What the hell were you going to do to me?" Bethany raged.

"I sure as hell wouldn't have missed." Travis gritted his teeth. His hand was sticky with blood seeping through his fingers.

"What makes you think I missed?" Bethany asked.

"You didn't kill me, that's what," Travis growled. "I would have shot to kill."

"Oh, you aren't going to be that lucky," Bethany told him." You're going to trial for the cold-blooded murder of a DEA agent. You'll spend the rest of your life in jail waiting for the state to put you down like the rabid animal you are!"

"What the hell are you talking about?" Travis searched her face.

"Ian Carter was my brother. I was there, in that alley, when you shot him," Bethany spat. "I saw you pull the trigger of the gun that killed my brother."

"Grayson's been looking for you ever since," Travis growled.

Bethany nodded. "Yeah, I'm the one who ran away from that alley. I'm the woman you ran off the road." Bethany kicked his foot. "You should have made sure I was dead that night."

The firing stopped. For less than a heartbeat, there was no sound. Bethany motioned Travis to his feet. There they waited. A couple more shots were fired before Ben yelled for Bethany.

"I'm around the back!" she called out. "I've got Travis. He's wounded."

A man came out of the woods with a DEA jacket on. His gun was trained on Travis. He grabbed Travis's wrist and yanked it behind his back. Travis growled in pain but before he could do anything, he was handcuffed. The DEA agent marched him to the front yard where more agents met them. Ben and Colton were already there.

Grayson was handcuffed, kneeling in the driveway. There was the body of an older man lying in the snow next to him. Bethany could see several bullet holes in his dead body. He looked enough like Grayson and Travis that Bethany easily took him to be Seth Trainer. Colton was OK.

Steve and the rest of his men walked up the driveway. The agent forced Travis to his knees beside his brother. When he saw his father's body lying in the snow, he turned to glare at Colton. "You're a dead man, Rivers. I swear to God, you are dead." Travis turned to Bethany, "And you're next. Even if you send me to prison, I'll find a way to kill you both."

"You'd better find a way to do it quickly, because you killed a cop when you shot my brother. They're going to give you the needle for that. It won't take twenty years either," Bethany told him. She straightened up to have a word with his brother. Grayson knelt in the snow. She caught a whiff of his aftershave on the wind. It was the same sickly over sweet scent she remembered from the alley. Yet not quite the same. Her nostrils flared as nausea overcame her. She had to back away from him.

Bethany told Colton. "He was there the night Travis shot Ian. I remember his aftershave. He was the man standing in the shadows." The wind shifted bearing with it the same scent to another quarter. She looked closer at the body lying in the snow beside Grayson then stepped closer in order to study his face. The face she had not seen so clearly flashed in her mind's eye. She gasped in horror. Turning to Colton she pointed to Seth's face.

"My God, it was his face I saw that night," Bethany claimed as she pointed at Seth Trainer. "He was there that night, too—both of them standing in the shadows."

"What?" Colton asked as he looked from Grayson to his father. "You saw Seth in that alley? Are you sure?"

Bethany nodded. "Grayson's and Seth's aftershaves were

blended together on the wind. Seth moved close enough to the light that I could see his distorted, raging face. When he returned to the shadows, he turned to someone standing beside him. He told that person he wouldn't go to jail because his bastard kids couldn't do something right."

Grayson struggled against his handcuffs. "If I had been a better shot that night, you'd have died in that alley."

Colton nodding, stepped closer to Grayson and Travis. His gaze held theirs. "If you try anything, I've got some friends inside prison who would be very happy to teach you to do better. If you take one step out of line, you'll find out what I'm talking about. You won't see them if you behave, but you cross the line, they will make you wish to God the state would end it. My friends will see to it that your life is not worth living."

Sweat broke out on Grayson's face. Travis spit into the ground in front of Colton.

Steve's group hauled Grayson and Travis to their feet. "We'll take care of these two. I have a special cell waiting for them." Steve, aware of Seth's lifeless body, nodded. "We'll send the coroner for him."

"I'll go along with you, that way Bethany can have the car." Ben reached into his pocket for the car keys, threw them to Bethany.

Smiling, she turned to Colton. "Well it looks like you have your ranch back. The bad guys are going to jail. Thank you for everything you've done for me the last few days." She wanted to say more but she didn't know how to tell him what she was feeling. She needed time to figure out how she felt.

Colton didn't know what to say. He could feel her slipping away and he knew he couldn't stop her from leaving. The silence between them was turning awkward.

"I suppose I should get back to town. There's a mountain of paperwork to get done," Bethany finally told him. She turned away, walking to the car and climbing in the driver's side. Colton watched as she backed up the driveway. He couldn't believe she would leave without another word.

# Chapter Ten

The next few days were busy ones. The Trainer brothers were charged with murder and drug trafficking; all the players were finally sorted out. The evidence the DEA recovered at the warehouse was enough to track and shut down a major drug artery. Fifteen people were arrested and when the charges were read, accused couldn't spill the beans fast enough on one another, all for the promise of lesser charges.

Bethany didn't have time to think about the days she'd spent with Colton until almost Christmas. It was on December 23 at the memorial for Ian that she finally thought about Colton. At the service when she realized only a handful of people came to pay their respects, she knew she didn't want to end up alone in life as Ian had. Life was too short not to go after what you wanted, and she knew she wanted Colton. She didn't know if he felt the same way, but if their shared passion was anything to go by, she knew she had to find out. She could still feel the sizzle from that kiss on her lips. Her whole body tingled when his lips had met hers. His kiss kindled something inside her. She couldn't help herself, she wanted to nurture that spark. She felt herself blossom in his arms, and she wanted to wake up in his arms for the rest of her life.

After the service a car pulled up in the parking lot and a young black man got out of the passenger seat. He smoothed his long hair, hitched up his jeans then deliberately walked up to Bethany. He said, "Hey man, I'm sorry I missed the service. Ian was a friend of mine. I wanted to pay my respects."

She knew who the young man was the moment she saw him. This was the mysterious Nick she couldn't remember until now. "Is your name Nick?"

The young man nodded. "I'm sorry about Ian. He shouldn't have been anywhere near the alley that night. I should have been there instead."

"Ian wouldn't have allowed that. I know if he hadn't thought a lot of you, he wouldn't have taken your place."

Nick considered that. "He died that night in my place. I don't think I can forget that. He took a bullet because I made an unwise decision."

"No, he died doing the right thing for the right reason. He saved your life because he knew it was the right thing to do. The only way he would have died in vain is if you go back to that way of life."

Nick shook his head. "That won't happen. Ian taught me better than that. He taught me my life is worth more than that. Because of him I have a chance to get out and I'm staying out."

"Then as hard as it is to accept, Ian died for the right reason," Bethany smiled. "He knew what he was doing that night. I followed him but I couldn't change the outcome. Neither of us could have saved him and nothing could stop him from doing exactly what he did."

"Did you get the man who shot him?" Nick asked.

Bethany nodded. "We got everyone involved in the drug case and in Ian's murder."

"Good," Nick agreed. "I'm glad that crap is off the streets. I started dealing before I knew what I was doing. A buddy needed some help delivering some packages. You know, at first it was easy money, but then when I wanted to quit, I couldn't just walk away. That's when Ian found out what I was doing. He took my place the night I was going to confront Travis."

She turned to see Kyle getting out of a car. Kyle Long had been a friend to both Ian and Bethany. In fact, the three of them had grown up together. Kyle was now a counselor for teens in trouble.

The fact that Ian sent Nick to Kyle told Bethany that Ian recognized in Nick a desire to turn himself around.

Kyle wrapped his arms around Bethany and he gave her a big hug. "Hey girl, I am so sorry about Ian. We would have been here sooner, but we couldn't risk getting in contact with anyone until we knew it was safe."

"I understand completely. We had Travis in custody, but he made bail before the D.A. could file murder charges. We lost track of Grayson for a while. Together they posed a very real threat to anyone who could connect them to the cartel." She turned to look at Nick. "Kyle," she asked, "is he going to be all right?"

Kyle nodded at the young man. "He's going to be fine. When I first met him, I thought Ian was crazy to want to help him. I mean he was a cocky little jerk, but when I got to know him better, I saw what Ian saw. He's going to make it. He just needed someone to believe in him."

Bethany's heart was gladdened. "Then Ian didn't die in vain."

"What about you?" Kyle asked.

Bethany smiled at him. "I think I'm done with this sort of thing for awhile. The job takes its toll and I'm burnt out. I'm going to find something else to do with my life. I know I want something more out of life than a lonely grave. Ian gave his life to help Nick, to fight the drug trade, to make a difference. I want to live my life with purpose too but on a different path."

Kyle scowled. "And what would that be?"

Bethany shrugged. She didn't want to say the words out loud. If Colton didn't want her to stay, the only one who would see her failure would be the woman she saw in the mirror everyday. "I'll let you know if it works out."

~ * ~

A few hours later she pulled her car into the driveway of Colton's ranch. The drive down from Minneapolis had been quite nerve racking. She was taking a big chance. She honestly couldn't predict what was going to happen. The butterflies in her stomach were starting to dance, but Bethany couldn't turn around to go home. She had to find out if Colton wanted her in his life the same way she wanted him.

When she got out of her car, she thought the house looked dark. She saw no one around the barns. The quiet of the place spooked her; it might have been deserted for all she knew. She walked over to the biggest barn and opened the door. She paused to let her eyes adjust to the dim light inside. She saw a man mucking out stalls. He glanced up at her and smiled.

"Are you Barry?" she asked when she reached him. He seemed like he was at home in the barn. She couldn't think of anyone else Colton would have working there.

The man nodded. "You have to be Bethany." He smiled again, leaning against the handle of the pitchfork he'd been using. Tipping his hat back away from his eyes Barry looked at her from the top of her head to the boots on her feet. He nodded his approval.

"How did you know that?" she wondered.

Barry's smile deepened. "Colton hasn't stopped talking about you since you left. I've been curious to meet the woman Colton was talking about all the time. Now here she is in person and I knew why my boss is so intrigued by you."

"Where is he? Is he here?" Bethany asked. The news that Colton talked about her to Barry gave her hope.

Barry shook his head. "He went off to the cabin this morning. He told me he had some thinking to do."

Bethany's heart sank a little. "Did he say what he needed to think about?"

Barry shook his head. "Sometimes Colton just likes to be alone. If you want, I can saddle a horse for you. I'm grateful you came to pay a call. I've been worried about Colton. I'm beginning to think Colton won't like to be alone for much longer."

Bethany was torn, though, not wanting to intrude. "Do you think he would see me if I did go to him?" she asked Barry.

"Why don't you find out?" Barry suggested. At her hesitation Barry offered a suggestion. "You won't know until you try."

Bethany nodded. "Okay."

A few minutes later Barry had a horse saddled and waiting for her. She thought she remembered the way to the cabin, but before she left she thought of something else. "Barry," she asked, "please don't tell him I'm coming. I need to see the look on his face when I get there."

"Give the horse his head—he'll take you right to the cabin. Colton has all his horses trained that way," Barry watched her ride away.

Bethany rode up to the cabin with butterflies in her stomach. As she made her way through the woods, she thought about all the ways she could explain why she had showed up just now for a visit. She still hadn't come to any plausible way to say what she felt in her heart when she saw the cabin in front of her. Before she would allow herself to think about what she was doing, she slid off her horse and opened the cabin door. Colton glanced up from the table. When he saw her he jumped to his feet. They stared at one another in silence for a moment then Bethany took a couple steps toward him. Before he could say a word she grabbed his shirt by its buttons and pulled him into an embrace. She kissed him with everything she had.

The kiss deepened. A fire lit up inside her. She could barely stand. Colton broke the kiss, looking deep into her eyes. When he saw what was there, he didn't hesitate. As their lips came together they both felt the heat of their embrace. He carried her over to the bed, laid her down and covered her body with his. Feverishly they pulled off their clothes as they kissed. When the moment was right, they came together, their joining unlike any other. Flames of passion consumed them both. The passion they felt took high above the earth until they burst, floating gently back to the here and now.

Later, when the embers were banked, Bethany said, "I thought about what I would say to you all the way here, and when I saw you, I couldn't speak to reason with you, as to why you should let me stay. I never knew love could feel this way."

Colton smiled. "I didn't know if I would ever see you again." He looked away from her for a moment, "Bethany," he faced her, "I was so afraid when you left that day I wouldn't see you again. I waited and waited for you to come back to me."

Bethany nodded. "I know how that feels. I had to wrap up the case and bury my brother."

"I wanted to be there with you for that. No one should bury someone they love with no one there for them."

"I had friends there. People who knew both Ian and me, people we worked with. Not many friends, but good ones." Bethany gazed up at Colton. "I found out who Nick is. He's a kid from the street who Ian gave a better future. When Nick showed Ian the shipment of drugs he was supposed to deliver, Ian sent him to our friend Kyle. Kyle took Nick out of town for a few days to keep him safe from reprisals from Travis. They came back the day Ian was buried."

"What did Nick have to say about the fact that Ian was dead?"

"He said that Ian died in his place that night." Bethany shrugged her shoulders. "He wanted me to know he wouldn't forget the sacrifice Ian made for him. I told him Ian wouldn't have died in vain if Nick lived straight. He promised me he would and I have to believe he will. He's working with Kyle now. He's going to be all right. He's going to be just like your friend Scott. Kyle will keep his eye on him. I think the fact that Ian believed in him gave Nick the push he needed to really make a difference." She shrugged. "Who knows, maybe Nick will make a difference in someone else's life."

"Sort of paying it forward to help someone else?" Colton hinted.

"Yeah, something like that." Bethany sighed. "I hope so anyway."

"What's happened to Travis and Grayson?"

"Travis is in the isolation wing of jail waiting trial for first degree murder and drug trafficking. The DEA doesn't want him talking to anyone. They will keep him safe enough to stand trial. They put police officers and other law enforcement personnel in isolation to protect them against reprisals from other inmates. Grayson is still in jail too. He will face federal charges as well." Bethany chuckled softly. "I'm afraid your Grayson found out that being a bully outside prison wasn't the same as being one inside the joint. He went head to head with a real bully and found out that a smart mouth isn't what its cracked up to be."

"What happened? I would have thought the same rules applied to Grayson."

Bethany shook her head. "Grayson didn't want isolation. He insisted on being in the general population. I don't know, maybe he thought he could get someone to follow him but it didn't work out that way. Let's just say he smarted off to the wrong person—he was taught a lesson he won't soon forget. He found out that without his gang of bad boys, he was nothing but a little fish in a much bigger pond. I doubt he'll make that mistake again." She chuckled. "He ended up crying like a baby. It's not really all that funny, but when I think of how he bullied his way around here, I have to believe God has a funny sense of humor. Grayson is on the other end of the stick now."

Colton nodded. "Maybe there's hope for him yet." He paused. "Maybe this is the wrong time to bring it up, but I hope you're going to hang around this time. I don't think I could watch you drive away again."

Bethany thought for a long moment then said, "If you'll have me, I'd like stay. I've had time to think about what I want from life. I don't want to end up like my brother. I want a home and a family, not a lonely grave with a handful of people at my funeral. Ian should have had a whole lot more before he died, but he died doing what he loved. He died making a difference. Maybe I'm selfish, but I want more than he had. I want the whole works. I want love and a man to make a life with, a family. I want it all and I want it with you!" She paused, blushing. "After a display like this, you'll have a hard time getting rid of me."

"Why is that?" Colton asked his words ragged.

Bethany blushed. "I love you. You showed me a world I could live in for the rest of my life. You have so much to teach me about life and love and I want to learn. You have compassion for people less fortunate than yourself, a loyalty to your friends and you aren't afraid of doing the right thing even when it puts everything you hold dear on the line. I want you and everything that comes with you, if you'll have me."

Colton snuggled under the blankets with her. "I can live with that." He hated to ask but he had to know. "What about your job?"

Bethany sighed. "I love my work. It's a noble profession. It's one that needs good people to do it but . . ."

"But what?" Colton asked with his heart in his throat.

"But I don't want to see the heartbreak anymore," he told him. "When Ian died a part of me died in that alley with him. I've buried two very good people who didn't deserve to die. It breaks my heart to know that they had to die that way. I loved them both but I don't know if I can go through that kind of loss again."

Colton hugged her close to him. He knew what heartache she was talking about. "Stay here with me and you'll be part of my world from here on."

"For how long?" Bethany wondered. Her question was important. She was willing to go all the way, and she prayed he was too.

"How about forever?" Colton asked. "I've never known a woman like you. I had no idea how my life would change the day I met you. You turned my life upside down in no time. I can't imagine living without you in it." Even as he spoke the words, he felt the embers of passion stirring inside him again. He moved closer as her eyes got big. She smiled a radiant smile.

"Forever sounds like heaven to me," he whispered as their lips met.

# The Prize

C.L Kraemer

The buzzing. What was that buzzing? It was near. Loud, irritating, continuous. Daniel Wilkes thrust his arm out and smashed his hand down on the radio alarm. Ahhh! Quiet. He began to slip into the nether land of warm dreamless sleep. It started again. That buzzing. Daniel roused himself from his cocoon of warm blankets. He'd have to get up. Leaning over, he shut the radio alarm off, swung his legs over the side of the bed, and yawned. Maybe he could call in sick today. There wasn't anything really important on his calendar. No, no, he couldn't. He'd have to go in today like every other day of the year because his particular expertise was pivotal to the running of his department.

His job as a computer repair technician was very important. He was one of the few people everyone was glad to see. When people called Daniel it was usually because their computer had stopped working in the middle of a very important report, or at month-end in the accounting department or crunching together a sales presentation for a new client. He'd come to their office, work his magic using his vast knowledge, and leave the hero. Rumors of downsizing in other areas of the company had processed through the company pipeline, but Daniel knew the upper management wouldn't touch the computer division, especially the repair department. They were the glue that kept the company together.

He wasn't so sure the new kid, Frank, was going to make it though. All he'd done since he'd shown up in the cubicle opposite Daniel was play computer games. Yeah, maybe he'd set up the company's updated new email system. Oh, and he'd set up an Internet website for the company, but site building was level one, social-networking-time-off stuff. Daniel's expertise was crucial, expertise the bosses on the seventeenth floor trusted to be scrupulous. After their last conversation, Daniel suspected Frank might be downsized along with the secretarial department.

~ * ~

"Hey, Daniel."
Daniel rolled his eyes at the sound of Frank's voice. "What?"

"Did you hear Becky in data entry was let go?"

"Yeah, so what? What's that got to do with us? They won't touch us computer geeks. I have the word of the vice president in marketing. Our department has saved his behind more than once when his computer crashed. He told me on the QT we *weren't* going to be touched in the shake up. So don't worry and stop listening to the coffee room gossip."

Daniel shook his head and started to walk away.

"Don't be so sure," Frank called after him. "I heard they're gonna get rid of somebody in our department."

*Last hired, first fired.* Daniel shook his head. *Poor Frank.*

~ * ~

Daniel took his shower, dressed then sat at the table in the kitchen nook. He really liked his townhouse. He was lucky his grandparents had thought so highly of him they'd arranged for him to inherit the place. He still snickered at the raucous scene during the family dinner when Gram announced they were moving from the old homestead.

His mother had exploded in anger.

"What! You're going to sell! But mom... the property is supposed to be *ours*!"

Daniel could tell the barely civil dinner conversation was going to wind into a whining tirade from the nasal tone of his mother's retort.

"How could you *possibly* do this to us? We *counted* on you giving us the house!" Red faced, she stomped away from the dinner table, snatched her purse, and slammed the door on her way out. His father was still sitting at the table, staring in disbelief, mouth gaping, at his in-laws.

Daniel had fought hard to keep from laughing aloud. He couldn't begin to count the nights he'd listened to his parents lavishly planning how they would redesign the "dated" house they considered theirs. Working to achieve the same goal never entered their mind. It was simple. What was Gram and Gramps was theirs by birthright. End of discussion.

Apparently not so.

Daniel had heard Grandpa and Grandma Wilkes discuss selling the huge home in which they'd raised their large family for three years before they put the house on the market. With a portion of the proceeds from the home's sale, they took the trip of a lifetime to Europe. Grandpa hadn't been there since the Second World War—"The Big One" as he always called it—and he wanted to see it once without having to watch for Panzers and ducking the Luftwaffe.

"Be nice to see what them German folks really look like. Heard them frauleins are pretty good lookin'; almost as good lookin' as my Nita," Grandad would chuckle as Daniel's grandma would shake her head and walk away.

"Incorrigible. That's what you are, Alvin Wilkes, just incorrigible."

They had left in May and returned the following September tanned, glowing, and fairly fluent in German. In the cab on the way home from the airport, they passed the construction site of new town homes inside the west edge of the city.

"Driver, stop." Al leaned forward and touched the man on the shoulder.

He paid the man to wait, and by the time Al and Nita Wilkes climbed back into the cab, they were the proud owners of a soon-to-be-finished town home in the city's newest trendy neighborhood. They retrieved their furniture from storage, moved into the townhouse, and set out to car shop.

Daniel's grandmother had spotted the maroon beauty on the car lot when they'd taken the cab from the airport.

"Alvin, that's what I want." She pointed out the new 2000 Thunderbird to her husband.

"You got your trip to Europe; I want to drive around town in style and *that* car," she pointed at the Ford as they passed the lot, "is the kind of style I want."

That's when Daniel's parents quit speaking to them. Grandpa passed away and neither Daniel's mom nor dad attended the funeral.

He'd come to play a vital role in his grandmother's life. After Grandad died, her health deteriorated and she never quite regained her former zest for life. Daniel made sure she got to all her doctor appointments, did her grocery shopping, helped her to clean the townhouse, and kept the Ford in good running condition.

When Gram made the decision to go into a nursing home because she'd nearly set the kitchen on fire with her forgetfulness, she asked Daniel to come live in the townhouse. She and Grandpa had paid it off with the profit they'd made on the sale of the big house. She willingly signed the title of the Thunderbird to Daniel when she moved into the assisted living center. The car had less than 20,000 miles on the odometer and was as breathtakingly beautiful as the day she drove the new vehicle from the lot.

Even so, Daniel had sacrificed to get where he was. He'd given up his personal life to cater to Gram but truth be told, he loved her dearly, definitely more than the woman claiming to be his mother. He often shook his head at how different two beings with nearly the same genes could be. But he couldn't get Gram to stop pushing him to marry. Visitation days always seemed to have the same theme between them.

"Daniel, when are you going to find a nice girl and settle down? I'd love to see great grandbabies before I die?"

"Now, Gram, if I have a wife and kids, I won't be able to help you as much as I do. You wouldn't want me to have to stop visiting, would you?"

He'd watch his gran sigh, shake her head, and smile weakly at him.

"No hon," she'd pat his hand. "I really enjoy having you here. Maybe after I'm gone you'll find someone special."

"Grandma! Don't say that." Daniel would frown and grasp her hand. "You're not going to die. Now stop it!"

The last time he visited, the nurse at the front desk stopped him.

"Mr. Wilkes?"

"Yes?"

"I need to speak to you regarding the notices we've sent to your parents about your grandmother's expenses."

Daniel frowned. "Expenses?"

"Yes sir. The home is... uh... increasing the cost for your grandmother's living arrangement and medical expenses. She's requiring more direct attention as her prognosis deteriorates. The problem is we keep getting the mail back unopened. Do you have their correct address or know who we can speak with on the subject of this matter?"

Daniel sighed as he withdrew his wallet from his trousers.

"My parents don't live in town anymore and haven't acknowledged my grandmother in several years. Her lawyer is handling her finances. Here is his name and number. He should be able to help you."

He frowned. *Will this affect me? Naw. Gram has made a provision I'll be able to stay in the house as long as I want. Right?*

~ * ~

Daniel smelled the burning toast as the smoke alarm went off. He opened the sliding patio door to let in some fresh air and was greeted by an icy blast. He dashed to the shrieking smoke alarm. Opening the front, he disconnected the battery.

"Blasted thing. Never works when it should and works every time you don't need it."

He grumbled as he took the blackened bread and dropped it into the rubbish can. He realized he was running late and wouldn't have time to eat.

"Man, this is turning out to be a bad day. I sure hope Nadine in accounting doesn't have one of her 'It's-Your-Fault-This-Accounting-System-Doesn't-Work' days." He blew out an exasperated sigh between his lips. "That's all I need."

He grabbed his overcoat and briefcase on his way out the

door.

He locked the door and, pointing the garage door opener at the garage, walked down the pathway. He reached the driveway before he realized the garage door wasn't open. Swearing under his breath, he pointed the opener again and clicked. Nothing. He stomped up to the townhouse. He heard the metallic rumbling of the garage opening next door.

He turned as a sleek red sports car gracefully slid out. Daniel stood transfixed. This was why he was sacrificing his social life. It was the most beautiful piece of machinery he'd ever seen. The mercurial lines moved the eye from the double horse insignia on the front over the barely waist-high roof into the aerodynamically designed tail end. The air wavered around the exhaust pipe emitting guttural hints of the power contained under the hood. The driver gave the engine gas and shot backward into the street. Shifting from reverse to drive and giving the engine more gas, the car noisily left skid marks on the quiet residential street.

Daniel trudged inside. He rummaged through the catchall drawer in the entry desk and found fresh batteries. Once the dead batteries had been replaced, the garage opener worked fine. He climbed into the older Thunderbird, lumbered down the driveway, and into the street. He toyed with the idea of leaving skid marks but changed his mind when he noticed a patrol car in the rear view mirror. This morning hadn't been a roaring success so far, no sense in getting a ticket. He was going to be late as it was.

Daniel pulled into the parking lot at work, stepped out, and locked the car. He looked at his watch. He was only ten minutes late. Considering this was the second time in all his years of employment, they'd probably forgive him ten minutes. He flashed his badge at the guard in the lobby and pushed the button on the elevator. Rocketing to his floor, he was walking down the hallway to his office fifteen seconds later. Inside, he hung up his overcoat and placed his briefcase on his desk. He hadn't yet popped open the latches when Frank came flying through the door of their shared office.

"You'd better get in gear. We were supposed to be in a meeting ten minutes ago in the conference room with the division manager of Information Services. Something big is coming down from corporate headquarters."

Frank made a cutting motion with his finger across his throat. "Move it!"

Daniel would have balked at Frank's histrionics if he hadn't said the magic words - *corporate headquarters*. There might be some truth to the office gossip he'd overheard in the coffee room. They'd find out at the meeting.

Daniel's plan was to slip quietly into the conference room without notice and take the nearest chair. When he opened the door, he was horrified to find all the seats occupied and people leaning against the walls.

"It's nice you could join us." Douglas Toland, the company President, remarked.

Daniel's cheeks flushed hotly. All eyes in the room were on him. He lowered his head, said nothing, and moved to blend in with the others leaning against the wall.

"As I was saying before our interruption," Ed Brody, Division Manager, continued, "there are going to be some changes and, I'm afraid, some of you will be leaving us. I'm not sure where we'll be streamlining but we need to tighten our belts. We're trying to work smarter not harder. We hired time management consultants several weeks ago..."

There were several gasps and terrified expressions froze on many faces.

"Good! I see no one detected them. Because of the reports sent to us by our consultants, we realized how much time and money is being wasted. In this market, we can't afford to give away money or business. Each of your department heads will meet with you individually. The results of the survey will be discussed as well as what management has planned for your department. So, if no one has any questions, this meeting is adjourned."

The happy chattering people who had entered the conference

room left solemn and grim faced. Daniel wasn't too worried.

*Oh, sure, I was little late for the meeting, but I've been with the company for thirteen years, right out of college. My progress reports have all been positive, and I've always gotten a raise. They wouldn't have sent me to the conference last year if they were unhappy with my work, would they?*

They needed the expertise of his field. That's what they told him when they recruited him before graduation. He couldn't really see how anything had changed.

The only person beside Daniel not fazed by the news was Frank. Daniel couldn't understand why he should be so carefree. He felt kind of sorry for the guy. Frank was one of the last to be hired. They were always the first to go.

Back in the office, Daniel checked his phone messages and, sure enough, there was his Monday morning call from Nadine.

Frank bounced into their office. "Man, didn't you read your email Friday?"

Daniel muttered something about being too involved with a motherboard problem to be reading mail on the computer.

Frank looked at him, "You don't know how to use it, do you?"

Daniel tried to ignore him. He gathered the materials he'd need to face Nadine.

Frank persisted, "You don't know how, do you?"

"*Alright.* I don't know how to use this system and don't see why I *need* to know. The old email system and phone messaging work fine. They've worked perfectly well for thirteen years. I'll be in accounting."

Frank shook his head. "You just don't get it. You're going to get left behind if you don't start trying to learn the new technology.

"I'm going to dig into the new project Mr. Toland has entrusted to me. I only need to figure out one more angle and the program will save the company millions in freight and shipping costs. It was so easy it was like stealing money. Capitalism is great."

Daniel grabbed his materials and huffed out of the office.

Daniel lived through the horror of Nadine the Accounting Witch, yet again. If they didn't find the glitch in her program, he was sure he'd develop a bleeding ulcer. He struggled through the rest of the day. Five o'clock finally arrived. The reception area was jammed with unusually somber office workers fleeing to the haven of their homes and families. Daniel envied those with families. They had someone to whom they could vent their feelings. He went home to an empty house.

He really had no one to blame but himself. When he'd first started with the company, his college sweetheart, then fiancée, had also been hired. After one too many nights of overtime, she returned his ring and quit the company. She'd gone back to school to become a dental assistant. She'd married her boss, the dentist. Daniel heard they had a thriving practice and three kids.

Well, he had this townhouse, Gram hinted she was going to will it to him, and he was saving for *that* car. Daniel steered the Thunderbird carefully into the garage, got out and closed the door. Walking to the mailbox, he heard the high-pitched whine of the finely tuned sport car before he saw it.

Screeching around the corner, the red beauty skidded into the driveway. The driver got out and stretched his long legs.

"Beautiful car," Daniel heard himself say to the neighbor.

"Yeah, it's an expensive toy my wife wanted. I'd rather have your Thunderbird," the neighbor said as he strolled into his side of the townhouses.

Daniel stood admiring the lines in the dusky light. If he had an expensive sports car, he'd never be alone. He was sure men who drove them had their pick of women, jobs, everything life had to offer. Sighing, he closed his empty mailbox and went inside. After a day like today, all he wanted was to heat up a TV dinner and relax.

Taking the hot tray out of the oven with potholders, Daniel maneuvered through the dining room and set the dinner on the TV tray in front of his lounge chair. He looked at the TV Guide. There was nothing worth watching. Monday nights were desolate unless you were a sports fan. He'd finish his dinner and read until he got tired enough to go to bed.

Weather during Indian summer was proving unpredictable. It could be cold and frosty in the morning and blistering hot in the afternoon. Tonight was uncomfortably warm. Daniel left a window open hoping for a cool breeze to stir the stifling air. The heat wrapped around him skimming across his skin but after tossing and turning, Daniel finally dropped off to sleep.

~ * ~

"You miserable excuse for a man!"

"You're right, I'm miserable. And guess who made me miserable?"

"Take your damned expensive play toy and go back to your hooker girlfriend!"

"Anything to get away from you, you witch!"

He awoke at three a.m. to the sound of screaming, cursing voices. He thought he was dreaming until he heard the blood-curdling scream. Blue and red flashing light strobed across his walls. He crawled out of bed to see what was happening. A couple of police cars were parked outside his neighbor's home. The woman was screaming and waving a knife-wielding fist at the man he'd seen after work in the driveway. He was shouting obscenities and lunging toward her, grabbing at the knife. Two large police officers were keeping the couple apart. Feeling confident the police had things handled, Daniel retreated to bed. He had to get a good night's sleep. Tomorrow, rather later today, his department was having the meeting the regional manager had mentioned. A good night's sleep would keep him at the top of his game to make sure he had all the answers the manager would need.

~ * ~

Tuesday, Daniel arrived on time. In the center of his desk, he found simple typed instructions for getting into his email. He followed the instructions. He was flabbergasted at the vast amount of communication occurring within the company on the new system. He realized, to his horror, he'd missed three different department meetings. *Why hadn't anybody said anything to me?* He took a couple deep breaths and reminded himself, *They really need me; they really need me.* They'd said as much last week. He'd be sure to stay on top of his email from now on.

The department meeting was brief. Each employee was handed a sheet of paper listing the problems found within their area.

John, the department head cleared his throat.

"Okay everyone. I know this is stressful for us all, but today's meeting is a troubleshooting session—nothing more. We'll start work on those items on each of your lists. Hopefully, we can keep from 'streamlining'," he used his fingers to make quote marks, "anyone out of their job. Please keep in mind you have to give 110% to make this process successful.

"I'll be talking with each of you personally to see where I might be able to help you bring your work game…"
Daniel groaned inwardly. John was an avid football junkie and never missed an opportunity to insert some kind of football analogy in his presentations.

"…to a higher level. Until that time, read the list and think about what's been noted.

"Now get back to work."

John smiled and with a flick of his hand dismissed the meeting.

Everyone gave a sigh of relief and meandered to their respective offices.

Daniel handled four service calls then finished his paperwork an hour early. He left for home. He'd put in so many overtime hours this week he reasoned if he left early using the time as comp time, he'd be saving the company money. Besides, everyone he called in the Human Resources Department, as well as his boss, all had their phones on voice mail. He'd make sure he got hold of someone tomorrow. *Surely that'll be all right? John said everything was fine today in the meeting.*

When he pulled into the driveway of his home, the red vision was sitting outside the garage of his next-door neighbor's townhouse. Daniel felt the hairs on the back of his neck rise. He didn't really know his neighbor, but what he'd observed told him this was not usual.

He started up the sidewalk to his home.

"Excuse me...?" the neighbor said.

"Daniel," he replied.

"Mike." The two men shook hands.

"Listen, Daniel, I've noticed you admiring my Ferrari," Mike said.

"Yeah. I'm saving to buy one myself. You know, a prize for sacrificing everything else?" Daniel answered.

"How'd you like to have this one?" Mike asked.

"You're joking, right?"

"No."

"I don't think I could afford it right now..." Daniel started.

"One dollar," Mike said.

"One dollar?"

Daniel was sure he'd wake up at any moment.

"One dollar and your Thunderbird. Straight across. I'll sign the title right now."

Daniel pulled out his wallet and handed Mike a dollar. He watched as Mike signed the title over to him. He recognized the name - *Mike Jacobson's Foreign Fantasies*. He'd driven past the car lot several times admiring the expensive European autos on display.

He cleaned out the Thunderbird and signed the title to Mike who placed a large valise inside the trunk of the Thunderbird and parked at the curb in front of his townhouse. Daniel slid behind the wheel of the Ferrari. The leather smell was intoxicating. He fleetingly thought about taking the car out on the expressway and opening up but slowly, carefully parked the beauty in his garage.

As he was closing the garage door, he noticed Mike saunter to the front porch of the townhouse next door and knock. A blonde yanked opened the door. He observed the animated discussion at the front entry. Even from his driveway, Daniel could see the blonde was furious. When Mike handed her an envelope and the dollar bill Daniel had just paid him, her face transformed into a crimson shade he had never seen before. He watched Mike belly laugh, bow slightly to her then turn and walk to the Thunderbird. He hopped in and drove away. The blonde glared hotly at Daniel. Turning on her heel, she went inside slamming the front door.

~ * ~

The following morning a large moving van sat in front of the house next door.

Daniel had risen an hour early. He dressed, ate, and hurried to the garage. Taking a soft cloth, he lovingly began to stroke the red beauty now parked in his garage. He still couldn't believe she belonged to him. After caressing her carefully to a glowing red, he climbed in and drove languidly to work. *Wait until the guys in accounting see me now.* All their jokes about him being a penny pincher would disappear. Frank pulled his Honda car next to the red beauty as Daniel was emerging.

"Wow! Who died and left you millions?" Frank advanced around the red beauty rattling off statistics making Daniel's head swim.

"Look, I don't know about any of that stuff. All I know is I like her, I've worked for her, and now I have her," Daniel gloated.

Frank continued to roll off statistics as they tramped through the lobby and up the elevator to their office. Daniel had tuned him out until Frank mentioned insurance.

"Oh, man," Daniel groaned. "I've got to call my insurance agent and let him know I've changed cars."

"Do you know how much it's going to run you?" Frank asked him. He shook his head.

Daniel ignored him. He had plenty of money saved and his outgoing expenses were minimal. Confident he could afford a fairly high insurance bill, he called the family's insurance agent.

When Daniel called and inquired about insurance for the Ferrari, Bob roared with laughter.

"Thanks, Daniel. I needed a good laugh. Now, really, what'd you get? A new Honda? An Acura? What?" Bob asked.

"Bob, I'm serious. It's a 1998 Ferrari. There's less than 10,000 miles on it. Can you let me know how much it's going to cost? Thanks. Call the figure to me at my office. I've got to go. I've got a full day ahead." Daniel hung up before his insurance agent could say more.

"I'll bet the only place that'll insure you is Lloyd's of London." Frank declared.

"Don't be ridiculous. They only insure one of a kind things like Betty Grable's legs or the Titanic or stuff like that," Daniel shot back.

"Whose legs?" Frank asked.

Daniel shook his head. *This guy is so young. What I need to do is start working on Nadine's accounting problem.* He was determined to repair her computer before the end of this week. He really didn't want to start every week with a visit to her office.

When the phone on Daniel's desk rang an hour later, he was deep into the problem.

"Daniel Wilkes." He answered.

"Danny."

He winced. Only his father was allowed to call him Danny. "It's Bob. There's only one agency that'll insure your car—Lloyds of London. And mister, it's going to cost you. About $500 base rate plus every mile over 100 will cost an additional $10.00 per mile."

Daniel groaned. It was a lot of money but state law required every car be insured.

"I'll just have to do it, Bob. I don't have a choice. You need a check now?"

"No. You paid for insurance on the T-Bird for the year. I'll just take what's left and apply it as a retainer on this new vehicle. You sure you're going to be able to afford this?" Bob asked.

"Yeah, I'll be able to afford it. I have very few expenses. Might as well treat myself." Daniel chuckled.

"I'll get all the paperwork in order and send it to the house. Bye, Danny." Bob hung up leaving Daniel feeling irritated.

What business was it of his insurance agent's to ask if he could or couldn't afford this car? Well, it was a moot point. He had the car, and now he had insurance. Daniel went back to the accounting problem in front of him. The solution was staring him in the face. He knew it. He just couldn't see it right now. Maybe a fresh cup of coffee would open up his brain cells. Daniel moved to the small coffee maker on the credenza and poured himself a cup.

"Need help?" Frank asked.

"Nah. I need to approach the problem from another angle, that's all," Daniel answered.

"Sometimes a new set of eyes can see what you can't. If you decide you want help, just let me know," Frank offered.

"Thanks." *If this coffee doesn't work, maybe...*

Setting his coffee cup on the desk, he answered his ringing phone.

"Yes, sir, of course. Right away, sir." He hung up the phone.

"I've got to see the boss." Daniel made the statement to no one in particular.

He strode down the long corridor to John's office. His mind turned over all the possibilities for this meeting. He realized at yesterday's meeting John had stated each employee would be met individually.

"That's right. They're just filling me in on what we'll be doing to improve our company production." Daniel relaxed. He was, after all, the only Computer Tech still here from the group recruited out of his college class. His expertise was indispensable. His knowledge covered the beginning of the company's computer changeover to the present. He knew what these programs could and couldn't do.

*Unlike Frank, who seems to think these computers are limitless. I know they have boundaries we can't cross.* Daniel knocked on the door marked *John Spencer,* Manager Information

Services.

A voice from behind the door instructed him to enter the office. Daniel took the seat offered him.

"You're Daniel Wilkes, right?" the manager asked.

"Yes, sir." Daniel would've been insulted but the company had grown so quickly in the last two years he knew keeping track of all the employees was impossible.

"Well, Daniel, this company is in the information business. And our department is the heart of the business."

Daniel nodded his agreement. That's what he liked about his job. It was the center of the company, which made him important in the day-to-day running.

"We've been receiving complaints from other departments you're hard to work with. Your attitude seems to be you're doing everyone a favor by showing up to handle their computer problems."

Daniel didn't understand. He'd just been doing his job— fixing their computer snafus. Sure he was a little—grumpy, now and again, but for the most part, he did his job and left. Now they were complaining? He was sure Mr. Spencer would understand his position. He was, after all, one of them. The Computer Guys.

"I'm afraid we're going to have to let you go. You've continually rejected the new technology set in place by Corporate. Your co-worker, Frank, has embraced the new technology and improved on the original. He's setting standards for this company I'm not sure many will be able to reach. We might have kept you if you'd taken a page from his book and worked on ideas and problems with him. However, we've had reports you're resistant to the changes the company must make to stay competitive in today's market."

John Spencer leaned over his desk and pushed an envelope to Daniel.

"Your final check is there along with a month's severance pay and payment for the four weeks of vacation you would've earned this year. I'm sorry, Daniel, but you'll need to be off company property before noon."

Daniel realized Mr. Spencer had ended the meeting. There'd be no appeal. Clutching the envelope, he stumbled down the long hallway to his office unaware of the activity around him.

*They can't fire me. I've been here for 13 years. I know all the old systems. They just can't!*

Daniel cleaned his desk of personal items and dumped his problems into Frank's in-box. *Let him handle Nadine every Monday.*

He picked up his briefcase, the few personal items he had and left. For the first time in thirteen years, Daniel felt like an intruder in the building he'd made his second home. The gloom would've consumed him but the moment he saw the car, his car, he brightened up. He'd saved enough money on his own to take six months off. Even with the expensive insurance, he'd not have to worry. Once inside the car, he opened the envelope. The figure on the check disgusted him. *I've given the company thirteen years of my life and this is all they think I'm worth?* He gunned the engine and, squealing out of the parking lot, left skid marks all the way down the street.

He'd show them. He had enough resources he could take his time looking for another job. He was experienced enough to pick and choose where he'd work.

Daniel headed to his townhouse. He parked the car in the driveway and noted the house next door was empty. His neighbor had moved out in less than three hours. There was a 'For Lease' sign on the front lawn with the number of a local realtor.

He dropped his briefcase on the entry table and shuffled to the kitchen to make a sandwich. He peeked out the window at the mailbox. The flag was down; the mail had come. He ambled to the curb, opened the door, and pulled out the envelopes. He noticed a letter addressed to him in his grandmother's elegant writing. *Great!* He needed some good news, and Gram was always good for a laugh or two. Her letters chatted up happenings at the nursing home.

He carried the letter to the living room and plopped on the couch to read it. She opened with her unique greeting.

*Hey there, buddy boy,*

*Happy Valentine's Day!*

*Just a note to let you know I've sold the townhouse to defray the ever-rising medical costs here. My lawyer told me to get rid of everything so the state will declare me destitute then I can stay. It's become my home, Danny. I don't want to have to come live with you cause you have your own life to live, after all.*

*Sorry for the short notice, hon. The new owners want to move in on the 17th. I know you'll understand.*

*Love,*

*Grams*

Daniel looked at the date the new owners wanted to take possession, the 17th. He had three days to move.

*What is happening?* He stared out his front window at the status symbol sitting in the driveway. He had to keep her. *But how?* Right now he didn't even have a place to live. Remembering the For Lease sign next door, he looked out and wrote down the number. He called. He choked when they told him how much rent they wanted for the identical townhouse next door; two months up front plus a cleaning deposit. It would nearly wipe out his savings. Even with his last check he'd only have a month to search for a job that would compensate him with a salary sufficient for the cost of the townhouse, the insurance on the car, utilities, food and car gas. Daniel had a choice to make—less expensive apartment or part with the car. His heart was set on this car. He called around. The affordable apartments were in the less desirable sections of town; places he knew he couldn't keep the car protected. Reluctantly, he concluded he needed to call Mike and see if he'd take the Ferrari and give Daniel his Thunderbird. He'd be able to live in a less expensive apartment and have transportation.

He dialed the number listed in the phone book for *Mike Jacobson's Foreign Fantasies.*

"The number you have reached is no longer working. If you believe you have reached this number in error, please hang up and dial again. Thank you."

He frantically phoned the information operator.

"For what city?"

"Austin, Texas."

"How can I help you?"

"Yes. I'd like the listed number for Mike Jacobson's Foreign Fantasies."

"Please spell Jacobson for me."

Daniel pulled out the business card and spelled the name.

"One moment please while I search for that number."

The silence was unnerving. Daniel felt his heart thudding in his chest and the palms of his hands were getting moist.

"Sir?"

"Yes."

"I don't have a listing for a Mike Jacobson's Foreign Fantasies."

"Are you sure? I have his business card in my hand! Check again."

The operator sighed heavily.

"Yes, sir. I'm checking Austin—no Mike Jacobson's Foreign Fantasies; checking West Lake Hills, Rollingwood, Oak Hill… no Mike Jacobson's Foreign Fantasies. Would you like me to check further sir? Maybe Houston or San Antonio, sir?"

Daniel shook his head. "No, thank you."

He slumped forlornly glaring at the phone. His life was a shambles. Even worse was the realization he'd done this to himself. He'd turned down opportunities at work to learn a new system because he was sure they wouldn't get rid of him. He'd let his desire for this car override his common sense. He should've realized Gram would need to sell the townhouse to stay in the nursing home. He been too busy being smug about how good he had it. Well, now, he was unemployed and three days from homelessness. But he had the car of his dreams for all the good it did him. He looked at the date on his final check.

*Happy Valentine's Day to me.*

Next time, he'd be careful what he wished for.

# Crazy 'Bout You

Clay Renick

# Chapter One

It started like any day in October. The air was cold, the sky cloudy. And Dr. Sara Aspen was getting ready for work.

She faced a mirror in her condo bedroom and was pulling a brush through her blonde hair.

"We're back to Mornings with Phil and Lynn," an announcer said on the radio. "The traffic update is on next but first a word with author T.R. Stallion."

"Thanks for having me," the man said.

Sara stopped combing hair and turned up the dial. A stack of paperbacks was on the night stand next to her bed. And they had his name on the cover.

Phil continued in the background. "You're in town for a promotion."

"That's right."

"The ladies will love this. You specialize in those titles with the half dressed couple on the cover."

"Afraid so."

"This book is different from all the rest?"

"Right." T.R.'s rugged voice stopped. "It's not finished."

"Well, that's odd," Phil said on the radio. "Did we miss something in the PR department?"

"Not at all," T.R. paused. "I've been writing about this for years, but really don't know much about it."

The other announcer broke in. Her name was Lynn. "I can feel a good one coming ladies," she said. "You can't see this but I've got goose bumps sitting across from this man and he's here looking for you."

"In a way that's right," T.R. said. "I want some input that will help me—as a person and writer."

"Let me get this straight," Phil added. "You want some lady out there to help you write—-your own story."

"Got it."

Lynn jumped in. "How will you find them?"

"That's the hard part," he answered. "I won't."

Sara dropped the comb. "What are you talking about?"

"She'll find me," T.R. said.

Phil and Lynn paused. "So," Lynn drew out her words. "They don't know who you are and don't know how to find you. But you want them to teach you something about love?"

"Got it."

"I've heard everything now," Phil said. "So how will they know it's you?"

"They won't," he said, "until I volunteer that."

Lynn began to shout again. "So we're going to have women all over this city breaking their necks to meet Mr. Millionaire romance writer who is now hidden but waiting to meet and fall in love?"

"Sort of."

Sara moved closer to the radio.

"Don't you think it's a bit unfair?" Lynn asked. "They have no way of knowing you're out there."

"You're right," T.R. responded. "That's why I'll leave a hint in the next few mornings and take calls at night."

"Where?" Lynn asked.

"Here on your program." He paused. "Don't you have a call-in program late at night?"

"I don't," Lynn told him. "But a local therapist has one."

"Great," T.R. replied, "I'll get some counsel on the side then."

Sara looked at her bedroom mirror again. A small newspaper clipping hung under it with details about her new radio talk show. "Local Therapist Starts Weekday Call In," the headline said. "Afraid of relationships?" the first line read. "One local psychologist can unlock the fears that hold you back... "

"So what's the first hint?" Lynn added on the radio.

"Patience," he said. "Today that special girl will have something to say about—patience."

"Well you've got it girls," Lynn told the listeners.

"He's out there. And he's looking for you. We'll be right back after this message so stick with us..."

Sara turned off the radio and looked through her bedroom windows out across the city.

*"He's out there, just waiting..."*

# Chapter Two

The office was busy that morning. It was on the third floor of a building that had mirror-windows facing the city outline and the river below it. Dr. Sara Aspen sat at a desk and looked through those windows. Her eyes were on the tree line that followed the river as it worked its way around the city.

Her reflection stared back. She wore a business suit and she had hair that was blonde, almost white. Her skin was smooth and features tight, athletic, ready to respond in fight or flight. It was the build of ancestors that went back thousands of years to Nordic explorers who sailed the world and explored the unknown. She was like them in a sense but her journey was inward and not across oceans. Her job was therapist. In that sense she both attracted men then left them in her efforts to help others. It was odd to develop trust in the safety of a counseling room then live alone.

But reasons extended to a childhood where her own father left for "other" women and she watched her mother struggle with her day care just to pay the bills. That was years ago but the memory remained. Sara Aspen was like other Nordic women who plot a direction in life and go for it. Even her desktop was clean, organized in neat piles of folders and correspondence.

Everything about her gave the impression of professionalism and organization. But there was no ring on her finger and no pictures of family.

Her thoughts were on the skyline when a voice came over the intercom:

"Dr. Aspen, your first appointment is here."

She sat up and hit the reply button. "Send them back."

"Very well."

The woman stood up and smoothed out the wrinkles in her business suit. She looked down at the first folder and opened it as the door opened. A man walked in, broad chest, narrow waist, muscled arms under a sports coat with short hair. His steps were confident, appearance clean: kaki pants, pastel shirt with coordinating tie. He looked like a linebacker from a professional football team.

Sara held her hand out. "Mr...."

"Stone. Blake Stone." His words were confident, tone oddly familiar. He smiled at the therapist as she pointed at a chair off to the side.

"It's good to meet you." She looked up into his eyes and smiled. "What can I help you with?"

"Oh wow," he pulled his hands together and took a deep breath, "what can't you help me with?"

"That bad?"

"Is now."

She waited. Her blue eyes scanned him for clues. They were clear eyes that understood even as they focused.

"I'll get right to the point," he volunteered. "I've got a problem with..."

The man stopped again. "It's so embarrassing to even talk about."

"Try me. I've heard it all."

"Not this."

"Well what's the problem?"

"I'm afraid everywhere."

"I see." She started to write and mumbled as she went. "Expressive social fear."

"I can't make decisions anymore. My job is on the rocks, girlfriend left, everything in ruins."

More notes with a whispered "Ambivalence, confusion,

frustration."

Dr. Aspen sat back. "That's it? That's all?"

He nodded. "Yeah. Happens at work. In stores. With women. I get overwhelmed and have to leave. The only place I feel safe is at home in front of a computer screen.

She took a deep breath. "Well that's really something that..." Sara struggled to connect her thoughts, "we can work with."

"Yeah? Really?"

"Sure." She tried to categorize his symptoms in her mind. "But first, let's start with some background info."

Sara opened his folder and scanned the page. "Says here you're a writer? She smiled with a raised eyebrow.

"Yeah." He nodded with a smile back. "But I don't want to talk about that."

"Okay." Her eyes looked over the page for other clues. "And you're from the coast."

"Right again."

"What kind of books do you write?"

"Please don't go there," he added.

*Sure, cause you just might give away your identity...* "So how can I help?"

He extended both hands with his palms up. "It's immobilizing my life. I can't do anything without this anguish over all the choices and people."

Blake's expression twisted. "I'll be in Wal-Mart and people get in the way. They'll stop without warning, block aisles with their cart. It's horrible."

*"You really do need help. I should've stopped for coffee on the way in this morning."*

"I'll be in the store for one item and get bogged down with all the options." The man stood up, his hands raised with the palms facing up—as if declaring innocence. Then his arms made chopping motions off to the side as if stacking cans on a shelf. "Forget tomato sauce. They've got diced, mined, strained, with and without herbs and seasoning, some that's chunky, others smooth."

Sara pointed at the chair. "Please stay seated." She looked at the file again and let her thoughts wander.

*I don't remember any of this kind of talk in his books. They were always about beautiful women and these hunks they would end up with*

"Take Starbuck's for instance," Blake continued. "I can't go in there and just order coffee. They've got a hundred kinds with all the added elements..."

Sara lifted a hand. "That talk about coffee makes me want some."

Blake took a deep breath. Sara scribbled something in the margin of his folder.

"My specialization is cognitive behavior therapy," she told him. "That means we would work on changing your thought processes to help you function with less stress."

"Sounds good."

"Part of that is what we call 'exposure' therapy where we will try to gradually introduce you to the situations that bring pain and discomfort."

"As in?"

"Anything with a lot of choices."

He leaned forward in his seat. "So you'll go with me while I struggle with some of these things?"

"Yes, exactly."

"Okay. When do we start?"

Sara looked at the clock on her wall. "A lot of your progress will depend on your willingness to take risks."

"Then how 'bout lunch?" He stopped. "I've got to make some changes fast. You said you'd like some coffee."

"I don't go anywhere with patients for safety reasons," she answered. "But I'll meet you there."

Sara smiled to herself. *He sure is playing this game well.* Her eyes scanned his chest and arms. *Well, I can play also.*

"So it sounds good." She closed her pen. "Let me tell my secretary."

"There's a place out by the by-pass called Bend in the River Cafe. He smiled and stood up. "If you can stand being with me in this melt-down."

"That's what I get paid for," she answered.

*This is going to be good. When will he stop the fake symptoms and tell the truth?*

# Chapter Three

Out by the river, the café was busy. It was an old cedar-wood building that looked more like a barn with a deck that backed up to the water. An old sign had "Bend in the River" on the front and inside there were the remains of horse drawn plows, pictures of old farmers, and tables with varnished wood. The atmosphere was dark with paneling, exposed beams, hanging plants that were fern-like and large windows that faced the river. Tugboats moved up the channel next to sailboats. It was a mix of traffic. And that also reflected the type of customers.

One waiter was looking through the windows at the water at that moment. He was over forty with dark hair and a thick day's worth of a beard. He also had the build of a swimmer but the chiseled eyes of someone who lived with pain. It was more than physical. It was an understanding that went beyond words.

Years had left the waiter with a quiet balance as if he could move around people and yet distance their emotions. He had one arm around an empty tray with his other elbow on the bar. A large white apron wrapped around his waist. But his eyes were on the river.

"Don't like this one bit," the fry cook said beside him.

The waiter turned with a glance. "How's that?"

"Your dad wouldn't approve."

"Why not?"

The cook was a large man with a stomach that pushed against his white apron. His hair was gray and arms thick. He looked more at home on the deck of a tub boat than behind a stove.

"The idea's odd," the older man said. "You know how he was about business."

"I'd love to ask him," the waiter took a deep breath and lifted his tray as he started off. "But I can't."

The room was full. Small groups sat around tables that were edged in the rolled hemp lines that ships used around bollards on a dock.

The waiter lifted a coffee pot and started through the room as the door opened and a woman entered. She wore a dark business suit and scanned the full tables.

The waiter saw her in the corner of his eyes and swiveled in mid stride. "I'll be right with you," he said.

*She's beautiful. Blonde hair pulled loose in a pony tail, business suit pressed without wrinkle, eyes dark blue and alert.* The waiter took it all in with a glance. He continued past tables as a gap opened in his thoughts.

*She's also alone, but the room is full and they all have friends.*

He stopped to offer coffee for a group of legal secretaries. But the image remained in the back of his mind. He set the coffeepot down in the center of the table.

"Help yourself, ladies," he told them. "I'll be right back."

The woman at the entrance watched him approach as he wiped his hands on the apron. The air smelled like cinnamon and cappuccino.

*Large eyes. Maybe a tennis player. But no expression.*

"Can I help you?" he asked.

She looked across the room and took a deep breath. "Yes, I wanted a table but..."

*Smooth voice. And yet sounds tired.*

He lifted a hand off to the side. "How about our deck. It's a beautiful day outside."

She smiled weakly and nodded. He started to grab a menu and start for the door but stopped.

"Will anyone be joining you?"

She followed and then looked out at the river as if caught up in thought. "Well, probably not."

He stopped. "That doesn't sound hopeful."

She smiled. "I'm used to it."

"I see." He continued out the door and headed for a table near the water. No one else was out there.

The woman sat down and looked at the sky, overcast now with a cool wind. Her hair fluttered off to the side and her eyes wandered across the water as sea gulls called in the distance. Then she picked up the menu and the waiter was still there, pen in hand, pad ready.

"I'm sorry," he said. "Would you like some time before you order?"

The woman paused as a dog stuck his head around the corner near the parking lot.

It was an old pointer with gray around his muzzle.

The waiter looked up and let his arms flop. "BOB...Get back in that TRUCK. How many times do I have to tell you?" He stopped and looked down at the woman. "I'm sorry. He knows better..."

An old lady stuck her head out the door with an edge in her voice. "You've got customers in here. You know that?"

"I'm sorry," the waiter shouted. He pointed at the dog again. But the animal didn't budge.

"He looks determined," the woman said from the table. There was a slight smile on her lips.

"Doctor visit and he doesn't want to go."

The old lady opened the door again. "WE NEED COFFEE!"

The waiter waved then pursed his lips with a finger toward the dog. "GET BACK IN THAT TRUCK NOW!"

The woman slid her chair back. "Want me to help?"

"No," he snapped. His voice then calmed as he looked back. "You're a guest."

She got up. "Where does he go?"

The waiter pointed at the parking lot as he started back

toward the building. "There's a beat up old Chevy out there. Just put him in the back and raise the gate." He looked back at her with sadness in his eyes. "I'm so sorry for this. But thank you for the kindness."

The woman whistled as she approached the dog. He was a short haired pointer with a tail that rose in a dip. That tail began to wag as she passed the corner and faced the parking lot.

"Well, Bob. How are you Bud-dy?"

The dog came closer and began to sniff. The woman ran her fingers behind his ears in a slow scratch.

"You're a calm dog-gy. That's good." She scanned the parking lot and let her eyes pass the row of Lexis, BMW's and SUV's. An old truck was in the corner like a leftover from a landfill. It had the rounded hood and rust from decades past.

She started for the truck, lowered the tailgate and snapped her fingers. "It's okay Bob. These doctor visits sound bad," she turned and stroked his head. "But they're over fast."

The dog wagged faster. His eyes were bright. The woman pointed at the back and snapped again. Bob jumped up and turned to face her. The gate was still down but she rubbed his head again.

"So what's the visit about today? Flea dip? Teeth cleaning?"

"No," a voice said from behind. "He's got a heart murmur."

The waiter was behind her in a jog. "They don't think he has long." The man lifted the gate shut. "But thank you for the help."

Another old lady was on the deck and started to shout across the parking lot.

"ARE YOU THE ONLY HELP IN THERE?"

The waiter turned again. "Fraid so." He smiled at the woman by the dog and started back for the café.

"We're trying to pay and there's no one else but the cook and HE DON'T TAKE MONEY!"

"I'm coming." The waiter rubbed his hands across his apron. "Look, how does an organic salad sound?" He walked backwards toward the café. "It's the best thing in the house. I designed that meal myself."

"Sounds good," the woman answered. "But why are you the only one working?"

"Easy," he turned and started to run. "I'm an idiot and gave everyone else the day off."

The woman walked back to the table. Her expression softened as the moments began to stretch. The waiter brought out a large tray and began to set plates around her: fresh wheat bread, large bowl of salad, coffee.

"Wow," she replied.

His actions were fast, eyes back on the building. "I'll be back later," he said. "They're watching me. It's madness in there."

"I see." She smiled and watched him walk away.

He glanced back and caught her looking. Both smiled.

She lifted the bread and took a deep breath. Steam came from the top as she dipped her knife in a pallet of butter and slid it across the top. It began to sink in a fast melt. She lifted it to her mouth and felt the blend of wheat dissolve in the butter taste.

The salad had spinach leaves with specks of cheese that stuck to the sides but not smeared. Each leaf had moisture from the dressing, olives, orange slivers, and cashews.

The woman dipped her fork in the middle and slid it into her mouth. The combination of sweet and sour mixed with the textures of nuts and olives. She let the savor linger and looked out at the river that floated by in spirals.

Later the waiter returned with a bowl of fresh fruit.

"Great, but..." the woman paused, "I didn't order that."

"I know," he said. "It's on the house."

"Well, thanks." She lifted a grape and watched him as she bit down. The skin gave way on with a tartness that was almost a snap inside her mouth. "I might need a doggy bag," she added. "You know how that is."

"Bob would approve." The waiter smiled. "He's my dog."

The woman looked at her watch. "Wish I had more time."

"Yeah, well...." He held the tray at his waist and continued to glace back at the building.

"So, could I get the check?"

"Oh no." He lifted a hand. "Not this time."

"What do you mean?"

The waiter smiled, lifted a hand, let it drop, pointed at the parking lot then back at the building.

"I take that to mean something." Her eyes softened again.

"Yeah. It was my pleasure." He looked at her and bowed with his eyes toward the water and then back. "But, a... thanks for stopping by."

"That is very kind of you then." The woman wiped her mouth and got up.

They both looked at each other then apart. She walked off and he started to lift the dishes from her table.

# Chapter Four

Later that night Dr. Sara Aspen sat at a table in the studio of WRVR and adjusted some headphones as a technician typed into a computer across the room.

"You know the format," he called to her. "I'll take the calls and send you an instant message or wave a hand when I need to interrupt. They'll show up on your screen as a list with the tag next to the first name."

"Got it, Mr. Harris," she said.

The man had gray hair and a silver mustache. "Call me Max."

"Okay, Max."

A large picture window opened on one wall to face the river and another on the lobby for people to watch. Sara let her eyes wander out to the water.

"Three minutes to count down," Max added.

"Sounds good." Sara slid out some notes and arranged them on the table in front of her. She wore the same dark business suit from the day but her eyes opened suddenly as if in awareness.

"What about our guest? We were supposed to have someone—right?"

"He called."

"And?"

"Hook up. I've got him waiting on line two." Max pointed at the phone.

Sara reached for her end. "Hello."

"Yes. Can I help you?" The man's voice was deep.

"You're T.R.?"

"That's right."

"I'm Dr. Aspen," She waved a hand in front of her face. "How are you?"

"Nervous, but I'll get over it."

"Well, the format is easy," she said. "We'll take some calls and listen. I've got some issue notes but probably won't need it with you on tonight."

"I didn't want you to change anything because of me."

"No problem." She looked up. Max was waving his finger as if to say "one minute."

"So how was your day?" Sara added.

"Horrible. And yours?"

"Bizarre. But then you can expect that in my field."

T.R. took a deep breath. "I'd have a lot to talk with you about."

"That so."

Max raised his hand. "Twenty seconds."

"The doctor's in tonight so what's on your mind?"

"I always screw up around beautiful women," he confessed.

"That so? What happened?"

"Today I met the nicest lady. She was gorgeous, thoughtful, and I couldn't even…" He paused.

Max lifted both hands: "Ten seconds". Some background music came over the speakers with an introduction to "Mental Health and You."

"Do what?" Sara asked with her hand cuffing the phone.

"Talk with her." T.R. replied. "I was frozen. Not cold. Just scared stiff."

Max held up a thumb. Sara held the phone off to the side.

"Welcome to the show," she said into the microphone. It hung from the ceiling just above her nose. "I'm Dr. Sara Aspen. The topic is mental health. And we have a wonderful guest tonight. His name is T.R. Stallion and many of you will recognize his novels."

16

She paused. Max pushed a button and pointed at the phone with a motion as if to hang it up.

"Welcome to the show, T.R."

"Glad to be here," he said over the speakers.

"To begin with, tell us about this experiment," Sara added. "I heard about it this morning when I was getting ready for work."

"Yeah," his voice was tired. "I wanted the ladies out there to teach me about love."

"That's odd coming from an expert." She smiled.

"I wouldn't be so sure about that."

Sara looked at the microphone again. "I've got a lot of questions of my own. I'm a practicing therapist, but I'll have to confess a long standing attraction for your work."

"You're too kind."

"Tell us about yourself."

"That's the dull part," he replied. "I want to tell you about a wonderful woman I met today."

Max held up a hand. A name appeared on the screen. It came with the word "Natalie."

"Hold that thought T.R.," Sara looked down at the computer. "We've got a caller already." She waited. "You're on, Natalie. What's your comment?"

"I didn't mean to back into you and leave in the bank parking lot today." Her voice was high pitched. "I really was going to stop."

"That wasn't me," T.R. laughed. "But I'm sure the police will want to visit with you."

Sara leaned against the table. "Confession is good for the soul, Natalie."

Max held up another finger. The word "Jessica" came on the screen.

"We've got another caller," Sara noted. "You're on, Jessica."

The woman's voice was smooth. "I saw you today," she whispered. "And wanted to, you know, talk more."

"I like the sound of that," T.R. said. "If you're the one I'm thinking about, it was nice."

"Tell us about it," Sara added.

"Well, let me describe the setting." T.R. paused. "We were near the river."

"That could be anywhere in 'river' city."

"The birds were out. The water was smooth. The wind set your hair off to the side." T.R. paused again. "It made the light pull off the water and across your eyes. I wanted to stand there all day."

"Wow." Sara took a deep breath. "Now you know how he writes those novels, ladies."

"And that's the odd part," T.R. continued. "I'm a total failure at love. I wanted to sit there and just be with you."

"WHY DIDN'T YOU?" Jessica asked.

"That gets back to my hint from this morning."

"It was something about patience," Sara looked down at the telephone. It was still off the hook. She started to put it back on the cradle but a caller I.D. was next to the receiver. And it blinked with the words Bend in the River Café.

"Where are you calling from?" Sara asked.

T.R. paused. "Why do you ask that?"

"I don't want you to give away your location or anything."

"I'd go crazy," T.R. confessed. "Really, I can't handle any attention. That's behind all the secrecy."

"My analytical mind is spinning now," Sara told him.

Max held up ten fingers and then pulled the index finger across his throat.

"Well, let me interrupt. I'm Dr. Sara Aspen. We're about to break. You tuned into Mental Health and You. Tonight's guest is the romance novelist T.R. Stallion. He's here for an experiment and will take your questions after this…"

The music came on again. Sara adjusted her earphones and sat up again.

"I'm sorry about that question," she said. "I just looked down at the caller I.D. in front of me."

"No problem."

"That's a special place," she added. "I had the best time there today."

"You did?"

"Yeah, I was supposed to meet a patient there. Of course they never showed up. They never do. But I met this waiter with an incredible dog. I didn't get his name but he paid for my meal. It was really special out there by the water."

There was silence on the other end.

"Still there?" she asked.

"Yes. I mean..." He coughed. "Wow."

"Do you know him?"

"Oh, him... don't know if I really do." His voice got weaker.

Max held up ten fingers again. Sara adjusted her headphones and looked down at her notes. Theme music came over the speakers. The green light came back on.

"Welcome back," she said into the microphone. "I'm Dr. Sara Aspen. The show is Mental Health and You and our special guest tonight is romance writer T.R. Stallion. I get goose bumps just thinking about your novels. Want to talk about that?"

He laughed. "You or the stories."

She squinted her eyes. "You know how to make a lady feel special."

"Well, I was talking about one I met today. It felt like love at first sight."

Max held up a finger again. The name "Stephanie" came on the screen.

"We've got another caller," Sara added. "Her name is Stephanie. What's your question or comment?"

The girl took a deep breath. "Well, I felt the same way today," she said.

"How's that?" T.R. asked.

"I knew it was you at the Quick-e Lube. You were so thoughtful with all those customers. I couldn't keep my eyes off you, especially when you looked in my window to ask about windshield wiper fluid."

"I wish that were me, Stephanie, but it wasn't."

Sara took a deep breath. "Sounds like some dynamics going on in that exchange." She glanced at the computer screen. Names began to accumulate in a long list.

"We're getting calls from all over. We'll get to some of those but first tell us about yourself. Some people may not read romance fiction."

"Okay." He said. "I'm 43 and single, have been all my life."

"That's odd for someone who writes about love."

"And I'm sure you could explain it all to me." He paused in thought. "I may write about relationships but I really don't know anything about them." He began to stammer. "I get weak around nice looking women."

"That's something to explore," Sara replied. "Sounds like someone got burned along the way."

"Yes and no. There were special ladies along the way but…"

"Something happened," Sara commented. "And it's still painful."

"Very much." He paused.

Sara glanced at Max. He had both hands in the air. "Let's take a caller. We've got dozens on the screen."

She went to click on one but a phone went off. It was in her pocket. She looked down and then at the screen.

"Go ahead, caller."

Sara held the cell phone and looked at the number: "Answering Service." There was a tag below it. "URGENT".

Max saw the confusion, got up and pointed at the door. "I'll take over."

She hit the on button and continued out. "Yes?"

"Dr. Aspen, this is your answering service. I'm sorry to interrupt but you've got a suicidal call."

"Sure. Put them through."

She continued outside into the hallway then through the lobby and into the night. "Hello?"

A man's voice came on with a loud screech. "I've got a gun pointed at my head. The hammer is pulled back and my finger is on

20

the trigger."

"Who is this?"

"Blake."

"From today?"

"Yeah. But you won't have to worry about that in several minutes."

Sara took a deep breath. The river gurgled off to the side. "Please give me a chance. Let's talk about this. Put the pistol down."

"Not on your life."

"Then at least turn the weapon to the side and release the hammer."

"No way."

"You're upset."

"Got that."

"Tell me about it." "Look, Doctor. I'm tired of all the pain. You understand?"

"Sure I do. It's getting to you."

"Just like today. I planned to meet you at that place today at lunch—but couldn't."

"There's more involved here."

"I'm looking in the mirror now. The gun is next to my head. I'm about to pull the trigger."

Sara took another deep breath. "Keep talking to me. Tell me about your anger." She looked out at the water. It made swirling motions with the current as it snaked along the edge.

"You don't know what it's like to live with pain every day of your life."

"You're absolutely right. I don't know about your pain. So tell me about it."

"I'm tired of all the crap. The lies. The jerks."

"Sounds work related."

"SURE IT IS!"

Sara closed her eyes and tried to concentrate. "You write for a living."

"If you want to call it that."

"You wouldn't tell me about the books."

Blake laughed. "They're procedure manuals. I work for the IRS." "And that frustrates you."

He laughed with a type of disgust. "Put yourself in my place."

Sara took another deep breath. "You want something better for your life."

"You wouldn't?"

"Listen, Blake. There's hope. You can always get another job. I'll help you but you've got to put the gun down. Tell me where you are now."

"I'm at home."

"What's the address? I don't have that information. It's back in my office."

"No way. You'll get the cops over here. They'll lock me up like a dog."

"Listen to me. I was just talking with a writer. He'd be glad to talk with you. Just tell me where you are and we'll—stop by for a chat. Please. Put the gun down."

"What will he talk about?"

"All about writing. He does romance novels. His name is T.R. Stallion."

Blake paused. "I heard about him." More silence.

"Just tell me the address."

"I can't take the big crowds anymore."

"Course you can't Blake. You live in a condo, right?"

"Yeah, number five at the hilltop."

Sara nodded and started back into the building. The lobby had a phone and she reached for the receiver with fingers that shook across the 911. Max was at the control booth on the other side of the glass window. And he was waving a hand at her as if to come back.

"You still there?" Blake said on the cell phone.

"Yeah, hold a minute," she answered. "I've got to scratch an itch." Sara then listened to the dial tone as the operator picked up.

"Emergency. Can I help you?"

"Yeah. I'm Dr. Sara Aspen. I've got a suicidal patient at Number 5 Condo in the Hilltop development. He's got a loaded pistol next to his head and he's threatening to pull the trigger."

"Hold while we dispatch a unit," the operator said.

Max had both eyebrows lifted as if to shout. Blake was shouting on the other end.

"YOU'RE CALLING THE COPS! I KNOW IT."

Sara put a hand up to her eyes and lifted the cell phone. "Blake, please bear with me. We can help. You've got to give us a chance though."

"HAVE YOU EVER WORKED FOR THE IRS?"

Max started to pound on the glass window. Sara waved back and looked at the other phone.

"Okay, Doctor, we've got help on the way."

"Thank you." She hung up.

"You said the writer was coming over with you for a chat!" There was a hurt tone in his voice.

"We will. I'll ask him right now. But you've got to promise me you'll stay on the line."

"There's a bullet in this gun with my name on it."

Sara opened the door into the hallway that led to the sound booth. The control room was dark. Max threw his hands up."

"There are only so many commercials I can run while you're out there in the parking lot," he snapped.

Sara lifted the cell phone back to her ear and sat back in the chair. "Blake, you still with me?"

"Yeah but not for long."

"Okay then." She put one of the ear phones up to her free side as Max typed on his computer and the theme music came back on for the show.

"What's going on there?" Blake shouted.

"I'm doing a radio show live," she said. "Okay, welcome back to Mental Health and You," she said into the microphone. "We're here with romance writer T.R. Stallion. Still there?" she asked.

"Yeah. I am."

"IS HE RIGHT THERE?" Blake asked.

"Yeah, I'm here," T.R. answered.

"Sorry folks," Sara said into the microphone. "We've got an emergency in the background. Ah... someone I know is upset on another line."

"UPSET AIN'T HALF OF IT," Blake shouted.

T.R. spoke up at that point. "What's the problem?"

"Can he hear me?" Blake asked. "Put me near the other phone."

A rumbling started on Blake's end followed by shouts in the background. The phone dropped.

"PUT IT DOWN!" Someone shouted. "Grab him Mike," a voice added.

"What's going on?" T.R. asked.

Sara took a deep breath. "Just a minute."

Someone got on Blake's phone and they were breathing hard. "Who's this?" they asked.

"Dr. Sara Aspen."

"You the one who called?"

"Yes."

"I'm Sgt. Mike Adams with the metro police. We've got your friend in custody."

"Thank you officer." Sara paused again and hit the off button on her cell phone.

"I need to explain, folks. I'm a practicing therapist and... someone I know was suicidal. He just called with a gun next to his head."

She looked at the clock and then the computer screen. "I am so sorry for all the interruptions and drama."

"No problem," T.R. said. "Sure hope your patient is better."

"This business is full of surprises." Sara took another deep breath. "Let's see if we have time for more calls."

Max shook his head in the corner.

"I'm getting the 'no' message. So we'll leave this until tomorrow night." She stopped. "T.R. will be back with us with more about his experiment."

"Be glad to," he said into the speakers.

Max lifted ten fingers and started counting down.

"I want to thank the 911 staff in town as well as the metro police for their fine job in stopping something that could have been catastrophic," Sara added.

Max had two fingers up.

"Thanks again, T.R. Everyone have a good night and remember to take care of yourself."

The theme music came on. Max got up shaking his head. Sara pulled the head phones off and put her head on the table.

"Hey, you still there?"

It was T.R. over the speaker. Sara looked up at Max.

"It's on autopilot," he said. "Commercials. No one can hear you."

"Yeah," she said into the microphone.

"You okay?" he asked. "That was unexpected."

"Welcome to my life."

"What will happen to your patient?"

Sara closed her eyes and tried to think. "They'll take him to the behavior unit at the hospital."

"For what?"

"Tests. Observation. Treatment. He'll be there for a while." Her eyes wandered out across the river again. "I better go check on him. It's just gotten to be…'

"Too much?"

"What a night. But thank you for your help, T.R."

"Sure you'll be okay? I'm worried about you."

"I'm glad someone is. But, a… I better go. I've got a cat waiting for me at home and it's late already."

"No husband or boyfriend?"

She laughed. "You really are a romantic." Her eyes softened. "But no, only Neil, my cat."

25

"Interesting name."

"It's short for Neil Young."

"Good choice," he answered. "The music really was better back then."

Sara smiled again. "I have certainly enjoyed our time together. I can see why the ladies find you irresistible."

"I'll let you go," he finished. "But please do something to take care of yourself. That's good advice for your listeners—but you need it also."

"I hear you. Goodnight, T.R."

He hung up. Sara slapped her forehead. "Blake wanted to meet him." She got up slowly. "Well, that will have to wait."

# Chapter Five

Darkness reflected off the water and glimmered in waves. T.R. Stallion looked out through the windows of the Bend in the River café and let his thoughts wander.

He was in the second floor office. It was an attic room with an old desk, faded leather couch, and table that rested against the windows. He sat at that table and let his mind drift like the water that passed his window.

*Don't go. She'll know.*

*And then what?* another voice countered in his mind.

*She's a therapist.* He argued within. *She'll put all the pieces together.*

The thought brought a sudden fear. T.R. could see himself packing up and sailing out on his boat. Back to the silence and openness of the sea.

*Why not spend the rest of your life alone?* the voice asked from within. *You've been hiding for years. It's nothing new.*

*Because she's different. That makes it worth the risk.*

*But what about your readers? What about all those people all across the country? They'll know you're a fake.*

T.R. took a deep breath. He wore a knit shirt and old jeans and lifted his truck key. He let it tumble in his fingers.

*She was tired tonight. You could tell that I'm worried about her.*

*So you're just going to make it worse?* the voice said inside him. *She needs rest, not more games about your identity.*

T.R. imagined himself alone in the hospital hall while Sara walked away in disgust.

*How could you do this to me?* she said in his imagination. *Why didn't you tell the truth all along?*

*Because I'm in pain,* he responded. *That's what it does to you.*

He let the moment linger. The key dropped from his fingers. Another thought came to mind. Sara was alone in the hospital with her head leaning back against the wall. Her eyes were tired and she needed to talk.

"That does it," he said. "She's worth the risk. If I lose everything in the process then it was okay."

And that's the way he found her—alone in the hospital ER, head back against the wall, the waiting room television on with a commercial about "scrubbing bubbles."

T.R. walked up and paused. Sara was still in the blue business suit, her eyes closed and arms crossed. No one else was around.

One breath in, another out. Slow movement from her chest. He took a seat across from her and waited in silence.

*Look at you. Overextended. Exhausted. Helping others and yet—beautiful.*

She opened an eye. Then both. Dark blue—penetrating. "What?" She looked up and stretched. "I remember you from lunch."

He smiled. "Just passing through and saw you sitting here alone."

She sat up. "I came down to see a patient." She looked at the clock then yawned. "They were going to check on him and come get me."

T.R. nodded. "You look tired."

She let her head rest against the chair again. "I am. This job is too much anymore."

"You need to take care of yourself."

She looked at him as if in thought. "Where have I heard that before?"

He noticed her eyes focus on him. He had Latin features, brown eyes, dark hair that was thick like the day's growth of beard on his face.

He pointed up the hall. "What's the story on your patient?"

She took a deep breath and sat up. "I haven't even been home today. This is no way to live."

"Your cat must be going crazy."

Sara looked at him again and focused. "How did you know that?"

*You idiot. Now she wonders.*

"You look like someone who would have a cat."

Sara got up. "Well, I do. And you're right. He's like everyone else in my life. They all want attention."

T.R. got up also. "Well, I better let you get to your—patient."

They both started up the hall.

"This is surreal," She mumbled. "I was talking with T.R. Stallion tonight when my patient went ballistic and tried to kill himself."

He smiled as he walked "I won't even begin to ask about the details on that one."

She reached out and touched his arm. "And the odd part is a connection between the two. My patient is a writer and wanted to talk with T.R."

"Of course the man is busy and can't be here."

"They never are when you need something real."

T.R. smiled at that one. "So the patient will be disappointed on top of the sorrow after trying to end his life."

"Exactly."

He stopped. "Then why not let me be T.R?"

"You're serious?"

"Sure. He'll be drugged up anyway. Besides, I always wanted to be a writer."

A nurse approached. "The doors are locked on that wing, Dr. Aspen. I'll take you there."

Sara paused and lifted a finger at T.R. "Can he come? We won't stay long."

"Sure."

Sara hesitated. "I don't know about this. There are some things to consider." She stopped in the hall. "Confidentiality. I can't breach that and let you see him. It's an ethical thing."

"But I'm just…" T.R. scrambled for words. "A waiter. Someone passing through. Someone who doesn't know your patient—or ever will."

Sara paused. "That's true. You're just a—friend. Someone who's acting on behalf of the therapist."

T.R. nodded. "An actor."

Sara smiled and nodded as she continued up the hall. "Sure you're up for this?"

T.R. tried to swallow. "You mean pretending to be a romance writer?" His jaw muscles began to quiver in a half smile. Sara was inches from his face. Her blue eyes were trusting and vulnerable. He swallowed again. "I'll try if it can help."

Blake was in a bed alone when they walked in the room. It was pale yellow with no furniture except a bed. His arms and legs were strapped down, hair uncombed, eyes upset.

Sara lifted a hand. "Hello there?"

Blake looked from one to the other. "Who's this?"

"T.R. Stallion," he answered.

"Yeah? Really?"

"Wish it weren't so," T.R. said.

Blake laughed in a sort of cough. "How's that?'

"Wow, where to begin?" T.R. smiled. "It's that artistic thing where you notice too much."

"I hear you," said Blake.

"The emotions are up too loud." T.R. looked down. "It's unreal."

"Got that right."

"I can't be in normal relationships," T.R. explained. "So I spend a lot of time avoiding people while I wonder why."

"Too painful," Blake added.

"You're right." T.R. looked over at Sara. She was smiling. "But you're fortunate to have someone like Dr. Aspen."

Blake let his eyes drift to her. "I just started with her today." He took a deep breath. "Guess I blew everything out of proportion."

"It's easy to feel overwhelmed," T.R. said. "Other people don't realize that."

Blake softened. His breathing relaxed. He seemed to be caught up in thought.

T.R. put a hand down to touch him on the arm. "So, listen now. Go easy on yourself, okay? We're here to get you through this. Things will get better." He stopped. "It's going to take some work on your part. But you'll be okay." He pointed a finger at him as if he had a gun. "No more talk about an early end—okay?"

Blake smiled. "Okay."

T.R. looked over at Sara. "I'll be checking with Dr. Aspen to see how you're doing. And I want to get together after the hospital stay." He stopped again. "There's a lot we can do to get you back on track."

Blake pulled at the straps. "I'd shake your hand, but..."

"No problem. Just get some rest tonight, okay? Things will be better tomorrow."

"Thanks for stopping by," Blake said. "I really mean it."

Sara nodded with a hand up as she started out of the room. "I'll stop by tomorrow," she said.

T.R. had his head down as they walked up the hall. His steps were fast. Sara hurried to catch up.

"Well that was quite a display," she said.

He turned. "I'm sorry. I should have let you talk more."

"No, it...sounded just like the way, T.R. would have said it."

She faced him. He took a deep breath. "Listen. I didn't come here to talk about myself. I mean, we've got a cleaning crew at the café now." He took a deep breath again. "I know it's late. But would you like to stop by for some decaf? I make it with whipped cream. It's really good."

Her eyes looked into both of his. "Well, sure…"
"Good. I'll meet you there."

~ * ~

The café lights were dim and music came from inside the doors. T.R. waited for Sara as she stepped from her car and approached up the sidewalk.

"Can you hear that?" he asked. "Allman Brothers. They listen to it all night while they clean up." He pointed at the deck. "Let me get them to turn that down and we'll sit on the deck." He stopped. "I'll be right out."

She nodded and started off to the side.

"Take one of those lounge chairs," he shouted as he continued up the sidewalk. "It's a great view of the water."

She walked slowly. The river was dark with swells from the wind. Autumn was in the air. The season was about to change with a night that could fall cold or hot.

Sara approached a lounge chair and sat down. She leaned back. Lights faced her from up river like stars overhead. She let her eyes close as the door behind her opened.

T.R. walked up with a tray carrying mugs, a bowl, and a blanket."

"Got you some fruit." He pulled a table over next to her chair. "That's always good late at night. You probably didn't eat dinner."

"How did you know?"

He lifted the blanket and wrapped it around her. "This will help." He set her mug and bowl on the table with a fork and napkin.

"I don't know how to respond." Her voice hesitated. "I'm not used to being waited on."

"But you need it with all the stress in your job." He sat back in a chair beside her and looked back at the building.

"Let me know if that music gets loud. There's only so much you can do with a cleaning crew from college."

He looked over. Her hands folded in her lap. But her eyes were closed. And her breathing was steady.

T.R. lifted both and set them on the table. Then he sat back and watched the water in silence.

~ * ~

Movement. Quiet swaying. That's what Sara felt. Water sounds washed up against the pilings with the cry of sea gulls in the distance. She rolled over and tucked the blanket up around her chin and then opened her eyes.

The horizon was light colored. She was still on the deck. A tray sat next to her with a pot of coffee, bowl of fruit and cereal, glass of orange juice and a note.

*Please forgive me for not waking you up. You were sleeping so softly. Enjoy the breakfast. I'll be back soon.*

She threw off the blanket and grabbed the orange juice.

*"What time is it?"* she wondered out loud and pulled the cell phone from her pocket. "6:55... A voice repeated the numbers within like a shout. *SIX-FIFTY-FIVE! I have appointments at 8:00.*

She stood up and pulled a hand through her hair. *No time to head home.* She swore. *No time for a shower. No time to get ready.*

She grabbed the coffeepot and poured a cup and started to drink it fast, then coughed. *That's what I hate about this profession. No time for myself. And everyone waiting for—my help.*

She rushed for the car then started back and lifted the note from the table. She folded it in her pocket and left as she rubbed her eyes and fumbled for her keys. The radio came on in her car as she started it.

"We're back on the morning drive with Phil and Lynn," the announcer explained. "We've got T.R. Stallion back for day two in his experiment."

"Glad to be here," he said. "I want to start off with a big thanks."

"For who?" Lynn asked.

"Dr. Sara Aspen."

Sara stopped her car in the parking lot. She looked at the radio dial.

"She's a wonderful lady," T.R. said. "Last night was an incredible experience."

"Well…" Lynn drew out her words. "Sounds like there's something behind that comment."

"There is," T.R. added. "We had an unexpected problem on the show last night. Sara, I mean Dr. Aspen handled it with professionalism and concern."

Phil sighed. "Well thanks for sharing that," he paused.

T.R. continued. "If you're listening now, Dr. Aspen, you got my vote."

Sara smiled as she slowed at the driveway and stopped before pulling out in traffic. Cars approached from both directions at a fast rate.

"But what's the clue for today?" Phil asked. "We've got ladies out there waiting."

"Yeah," T.R. answered. "Today it's kindness. I'll be waiting for some help in that."

Sara tried to ease out and slammed on brakes. A line of cars wouldn't let her start.

"Give me a break!" she shouted. "I need a bathroom." She looked in the rearview mirror. Her make up was smeared. "Can't believe I slept outside." She glanced at the road again and gunned out into the line of cars. "There's not even time to change clothes…"

Her secretary was looking down when she walked in. "Good morning, doctor." She then looked up. "Wow. What happened to you?"

"Long story. Any calls?"

The woman had long blond hair and a peach colored shirt under a jacket. "No offense, but did you sleep in your clothes?"

Sara took a deep breath. "Who's on the list today? I'm not in any mood for anything strange."

"Well," the secretary looked down and then bit her lip, "we're starting with—Jeffery."

"No, please..." Sara rested her head on the counter. "I can't take much more of this." She looked at the clock and then down at the schedule. "Who put him first on the list?"

"You did."

"Why would I do that?..." She closed her eyes.

The secretary looked at the door across the hall as if into the next office. "You can always refer to—Dr. Wilson."

"No, Bret has enough problems of her own." She paused. "Okay, send him back when he gets here."

Sara walked slowly into her office then looked back. "I fell asleep on a dock. Long story."

Jeffery arrived ten minutes later. Sara was at her desk and tried to wipe the make up out of her eyes. He walked in with large glasses, dress pants, and a bow tie. His hair was bright red and stood up. His shirt was dark blue.

Sara pointed at the chair. "How are you?"

He looked over his glasses. "Forget me. What happened to you?"

"Long story." She opened his folder. "How was your week?"

No answer.

"Come on, Jeff." She scanned the page. "We've been working on your tongue issues."

"You're looking at my tongue now."

"No, I'm not."

"I can see your eyes."

"Jeff, I can't see straight. It was a long night."

"I see."

Sara paused to read the notes in front of her. "We had some homework for you."

"Didn't do it."

"You've been complaining about your girlfriend. It seems you can't go out anymore because of the fears."

Jeff leaned closer. "They're all the same. They stare at my

tongue."

Sara felt her jaw tighten. "Let's look at that."

"MY TONGUE!"

"No, your assumptions."

He leaned in and widened his eyes. "It's coming back on me." His jaw locked down, lips opening over the clenched teeth. "I can't force this."

"Would it help if I turned away? I'm not looking at your tongue. How about if I face the window and you can talk without any worries?"

She spun in her chair and sighed as she scanned the city below, river winding like a ribbon, sea gulls in flight over a fishing boat heading in.

*He's out there. We'll talk again tonight.*

"Well, to start with…" Jeff had a shrill tone, "I don't like anchovies."

"What does that have to do with anything?"

He bunched up his fingers in front of his face. Sara could see it in the reflection of the window.

"I hate them on pizza. They squirm with their little rotten eyes looking up at you…"

*Please God,* she prayed, *you've got to help me today. It's getting to me.*

"So, I'm sitting there with Janice," Jeff continued. "She's my girlfriend. And she orders this strange combination of toppings on a pizza. I felt like hurling on the spot. But I looked out at the window and Janice was starring at my tongue. Really."

"WHAT IS IT ABOUT YOUR FRIGGING TONGUE?" Sara spun in the chair. "REALLY! GET OVER IT MAN."

Jeff sat without movement. "You okay today?"

She threw her pen down. "No." Her hands shook as she shut his folder. "So, I'm going to suggest something very unprofessional."

Jeff didn't move.

Sara stood up. "Stick out your tongue."

"You serious?"

She leaned across the desk and gritted her teeth. "DO IT!"

He swallowed hard and stuck the tip out half an inch.

"More."

He pointed the rest at her.

She raised her eyebrows, eyes wide open. "Was that so bad?"

"No." He kept the tongue out.

"You're still breathing—right."

He nodded, tongue flapping.

"OKAY THEN." Sara began to soften. "This is not the issue." She stood up and started out. "I've got to get some coffee, Jeff. Want some?"

He shook his head. The tongue was still out.

The secretary had a phone in her hand and lifted it at her as Sara passed. "For you."

Sara covered the mouthpiece. "Anything fresh in the coffee pot?"

"No."

Her face squinted again. She lifted the phone. "Dr. Aspen. Can I help you?"

"Yeah." It was T.R.

"Well, hello… stranger."

"Please forgive me for calling you at work."

"I heard that comment on the show this morning." She smiled.

"I meant every word of it."

"Say, are you going to be in the studio tonight?"

"Listen, I know you're busy, but I've got to ask you something."

Sara leaned on the counter and covered the phone, one eye back at the office door where Jeff waited. "What is it?"

"There's this girl."

"Oh."

"Just met her."

Sara exhaled with a lean forward. "How nice."

"I'm head over heels, but can't bring myself to—tell her. I just get caught up in knots."

"Well… there's a lot we could work on. I've got a patient waiting on me. A…what's her name?"

"You'd love her."

"That so?"

His voice dropped. "I'm sorry to interrupt your work. This is so new for me. I've been single all along and…" He stopped. "Can I talk with you about this later?"

"Yeah," she whispered. "Sure. I'd like to get your perspective on someone I met recently."

"Really."

"Just happened." She put her hand up to her head. "It's crazy but I don't even know his name."

"Where did you meet him?"

"This café at the river. I think he owns the place. Every time I've been there he goes out of his way to be so thoughtful."

"Lucky man," T.R. whispered. "What would you like my input on?

"What goes through your mind when you first meet people."

"Sounds good."

"Is that the sense you get when you write?"

"Sometimes," he said. "I'd be glad to talk about it later."

"Stop by the station tonight," she stopped. "I've been wanting to meet you. I've got this mental picture after our conversations."

"I'll be with the girl… but thanks."

"You're still calling, though—right? You do plan to link up during the show."

"Wouldn't miss it.""Well, thanks for calling." She hung up the phone and felt a deep sense of tiredness that moved throughout her head and body. It was like the current of a river. And it didn't stop throughout the day until she opened the front door of her own condo and looked in.

~ * ~

"Neil...." She looked into the living room. It was spotless with new leather furniture, silver framed modern pictures, and large glass doors that opened onto a porch that faced the city and river in the distance.

The condo was on the ground floor with a small backyard that dropped in a slight slope with a view without fencing. Harwood groves scattered down the slope toward the city like a ribbon of yellow and orange. Autumn was picking up speed with the sound of leaves falling, scattering and scraping like brown snow.

Sara released the lock on the glass door and slid it open. "NEIL!"

A slight breeze entered the room. It smelled like hickory and oak. She took a deep breath and turned. The cat stuck his head around the corner of her bedroom.

He moved closer, tail up and twitching. The cat was white with long fur and an awareness that saved him from encounters with dogs outside.

"Hey, Bud," she leaned down and scratched the back of his ears. "Sorry, I've been gone."

She lifted the cat and moved into the kitchen with a glance at the floor. "Look at you.... out of food and almost," she lifted the water bowl and poured it out in the sink, "out of water."

She filled it and opened the cabinet where she reached in and scooped out some dry food. Sara filled his dish and set it down while she walked into the bedroom and started to unbutton her shirt.

The cat watched her movements from the kitchen as he dipped his head into the food bowl and began to eat. Sara went into the bedroom, opening and closing drawers then turned on the shower. The cat continued to eat but glanced up as he chewed.

The glass door was still open in the living room.

# Chapter Six

T.R. was at the café. He wore khaki dress pants and a blue knit shirt. A large box sat open on the counter as he lifted several containers inside: plastic mugs of coffee, bowls of salad, wrapped sandwiches. The fry cook watched him with both arms crossed over his chest and a spatula in one hand.

"You're not acting like yourself," the cook said.

"As in?"

He pointed a spatula at the box. "Pic-nic?"

"What's wrong with that?" T.R. closed the box. "She's too busy to cook a meal. Why not drop one by?"

"You media people crack me up." The cook lifted a hand, removed his paper hat, and ran his fingers across his gray hair. "Here the woman's got a radio show and you show up with—goodies."

T.R. lifted the box and looked back. "Do me a favor, okay? Turn on that radio in the kitchen. Listen while you work. You just might learn something."

The cook nodded with a smile that turned into a head shake. He started back into the kitchen. "Whatever."

T.R. placed the box in the front of his truck. Bob was in the back, tail wagging, mouth open, eyes alert.

"No," T.R. looked back. "You've been fed already."

He climbed in and started up. The voices inside his head were already talking as if in conversation with Sara.

*Wow, thanks for the meal!*

*It was nothing, really.*

*You're so thoughtful.*
*Well, I've been thinking about you.*

There was one car in the radio station parking lot when T.R. arrived. He got out and lifted the box as he walked in, eyes scanning the windows.

Only Max was in the control room. He had some ear phones on with a dark sweater that bulged in the middle. But he saw the box, lifted an eyebrow, and came out in the lobby.

"Smells great," he said, ear phones hanging from his neck. "Is that for me?"

"Well, I really brought it for Sara. Is she around?"

Max shook his head and looked up at the clock. "No, but it's getting close. We're on in 20 minutes."

"Great." T.R. looked down. "She's usually on time isn't she?"

"Always."

"Think she's at her office?"

"You can call." Max slid the ear phones back in place. "Let me know if you hear anything."

T.R. slid a cell phone out of his pocket and hit speed dial.

A mechanical voice answered. "You have reached the office of Dr. Sara Aspen. Our office is closed. If you have an emergency, please stay on the line."

T.R. paused. Another voice picked up. "Dr. Aspen's answering service."

"Yeah, I'm a friend and need to talk with the doctor. Can I call her at home?"

"What's your name?"

T.R. paused. "Trent."

"I'm looking at her list and don't see that."

"Is her number in the book?"

"No, it's unlisted."

"Where does she live?"

"We can't give that out."

T.R. clenched his jaw and looked back into the sound booth.

"Fine, thanks."

He hung up and tapped on the glass. Max lifted the ear phones and walked over to the door.

"Yeah?"

"What's her home number? I'll call."

"Don't know. The secretaries would have that but everyone is gone now."

"Address?"

"Believe she lives out in the Alcove," he stopped and watched the confusion on T.R.'s face. "Group of condos on the slope."

"Which one?"

Max smiled and then eased his expression. "Wish I could be more help."

~ * ~

Sara had a towel on her hair with a bathrobe wrapped and tied at her waist when she stepped from the bathroom. The apartment was cold with a wind that came from the living room.

"I forgot to close that," she whispered.

Neil was looking at her from the kitchen and his back was tense. His eyes went from her to the couch and then back again. Sara saw that and stopped. Something was wrong. She could feel it.

A shadow appeared on the wall of her living room. And it moved as the cat ran from the kitchen.

Her heart began to pound. The shadow moved again and a man appeared in the doorway.

It was Blake in a white lab coat, green scrub pants, and surgical white cap on top of his head. He also carried a small box.

"Hello, doctor," he smiled.

"How did you get out?"

He lifted one arm. "Creativity. Happens when you get a lot of time on your hands."

"What's in the box?"

He smiled. "Bomb."

"What do you want?"

"Answers."

"You are crazy."

"No," he came closer. "Just tired of lies."

Her breathing quickened, eyes flickering as if to gather data. "What do you really want?"

"A talk." He stepped closer. "You, me, and the writer."

"That's just a box."

He opened the lid. Several batteries connected to plastic pouches and wires in a tangled mass. "Want to find out?"

"No. Listen, there's a better way to handle this."

Blake backed out. "Have a seat out here. This could be a long night."

~ * ~

T.R. pulled around corners and accelerated the old truck. The box sat beside him as the Chevy strained under the need for speed.

*You're overdoing this. Rushing out to her house when she's probably on her way to the station.*

*So I'll look like a fool.* He responded.

*You already do. Calling her every chance. Dropping by all the food and coffee. What are you after?*

He pulled at the wheel as the Chevy began to lean on a curve that started upward. *Where do these ideas come from?*

*Look at yourself,* the voice added. *Pretending to be someone you're not.*

*As in?*

*Mr. Writer. When will you tell the truth about that?*

T.R. scanned the road ahead and saw the Alcove entrance. He pushed the accelerator to the floor and tried to force a plan into his mind.

*Answer the question,* the voice said from within.

*I've got to find her house...* He turned into the driveway as an image came to his mind. Sara was at her door in a business suit and was about to leave when he came running up with his "box" of goodies.

*How did you know I lived here? This is getting creepy.*

*Well I was worried when you didn't show up at the station.* He said in the daydream. *You see I'm a fake. And I need to be honest.*

The woman walked past him in the daydream and then climbed into her car with a strange expression. T.R. imagined himself standing at her door with a foolish look on his face.

Other images came to mind from the past: his Italian parents on the deck of their sailboat, hallways at new schools. There was always a new town to adjust to before they moved on to other shorelines or storms at sea. The movement left him off balance and awkward.

*Why can't we be like other people*, he remembered asking his mother when he was small. *Live in a house. Have friends.*

*Because we're on the way to something better, she told him. Your father is a master carpenter and this boat was his dream.*

*Why can't he work like other carpenters,* he remembered asking her as he looked up. *On dry ground—in a building that we can live in...*

He remembered her smile as she pulled him in an Italian mother hug. *We will. Soon as we find it.*

T.R. slowed to look at all the cars. The condos were in clusters with large amounts of pavement between them.

*This is crazy. I don't even know where to start looking.*

Even the cars looked similar. He stopped and squinted to remember her car.

*Nothing but a blank...*

His own parking lot came to mind at the café. He remembered the night before when Sara fell asleep on the deck and he left early for the radio station. There was only his truck in the lot that morning with hers across the pavement. He began to fill in the details in his mind when Bob barked in the back of the truck.

T.R. stopped the truck as a cat appeared off to the side between two cars.

*No way. She did have a cat, but... Sara's not the kind to just let it run free.*

And yet he looked back in the rear view mirror and saw it: Sara's car.

He pulled in and got out the box.

~ * ~

Blake was on the couch when a knock started on the door. He looked at Sara and then down at the box.

"Go on," he motioned. "But one pull of the trip wire and we're all history."

She nodded and got up from the chair. Blake saw the door open a crack with Sara standing in the narrow opening.

"Sorry to bother you right now," the voice said.

"How did you know where I live?"

"Well, I didn't. I stopped by the station with this." He paused. "Max said you were late for your radio show."

"Look, I'm busy." Her voice was sharp. "That's a nice gesture but..."

Blake got up and pulled the door open. "Well, look who's here—the very person I wanted over."

He waved a hand in and kept the bomb extended in his other hand.

"Why are you asking him into my house?" Sara kept the door open.

Blake paused. "Both of you said you were coming by to see me at the hospital."

T.R. remained frozen, eyes moving from Blake in the hospital uniform to the towel on Sara's head then to her bathrobe. His eyes were wide with questions.

"I need to confess something," Sara continued back to Blake. "This is not who you think."

Blake wrinkled his forehead. "What are you saying? There's MORE LIES?"

T.R. extended a hand. "I hate to interrupt anything, but I need to come clean also."

Blake and Sara snapped their heads in his direction. Sara spoke up and lifted a hand as if to block him.

"I don't even know your name." She turned to Blake. "He came from a café out by the river and stopped by that night I went by to see you in the hospital. There was no famous writer around so this guy offered to pretend and I let him."

Blake opened his mouth wider. "He's not who I thought?"

"JUST LET HIM GO!" Sara shouted. "Your problem is with me."

"No way," T.R. pushed deeper into the hall and closer to Sara. "I've got to tell both of you something. I didn't plan to do this now, but I've got to come clean."

"PLEASE DO!" Blake said.

Sara clenched her jaw and tried to push T.R. back out the door. Her body was up against his in a shove that pushed him and his box into the door frame. "Go back to the café, OKAY. This is NONE of your business."

"NOT SO FAST," Blake held up the box and started to undo the top lid.

"HE'S GOT A BOMB," she snapped at T.R. "I tired to get you to leave but you didn't listen."

Blake motioned with his head for T.R. to close the door. "Both of you step in here and sit down. We've got a lot to talk about."

T.R. shut the door and followed them both with the crushed box of food still in his arms. His mind took in the details: scrub pants and lab coat, small box with wires.

"Look," he said to both. "I've got to say this right now."

Sara lifted both hands. "Go ahead now that you're involved in something that could take BOTH OF OUR LIVES."

He watched her sit back in a leather chair with the white

bathrobe and her head still wrapped in a towel. "I didn't want to say this yet."

"OUT WITH IT MAN! WE DON'T HAVE ALL DAY." Blake looked from one to the other.

"Okay," he swallowed and looked at Sara again. "I am T.R. Stallion."

"No..." She glanced up him and let her eyes drift. "No way. I would have known."

"I didn't want to say anything because I've got these feelings for you."

Blake looked at her and then at T.R. "What do you have to say about that?"

Sara took a deep breath. "So you were playing some sick game all along where you pretended to be Mr. Nice at the café and Joe Writer on the radio who was looking for some special woman to teach him all about LOVE."

"Well, yes and no."

She took the towel off her head and threw it at T.R. Blake and missed. Sara then picked up a book off the table and heaved that also. Pages flapped open in mid flight. "You jerk," she got up and started for Blake. "Give me that bomb. I've got someone I want to use it on."

He turned away. "No, not yet." A smile crossed his face as Sara looked back at T.R. and then covered her eyes and left the room, her wet hair now disheveled.

"Where are you going?" T.R. asked.

"TO GET DRESSED," she snapped back at him. "DO YOU MIND?"

"No," T.R. took a deep breath. "Look, I didn't mean any harm." He looked at Blake. "I was going to tell her later this week..."

"I see lies everywhere," Blake answered. "That's what set me off. Both of you said you were heading back to see me today."

T.R. listened and let his eyes widen as if linking the events. "What's this all about?" he asked.

"You can't trust anyone anymore."

T.R. took a deep breath and looked down at his own box. "Hey, you hungry. I brought this for Sara but," he looked up at her closed door. "She may never talk to me again."

"What have you got in there?"

T.R. lifted out the coffee, sandwiches, and fruit bowls and handed one of each to the odd looking man in a doctor's uniform.

Blake opened the wrapper. "Club sandwiches on wheat, my favorite." He sat back on the couch and opened the lid on the coffee. "Got any cream and sugar?"

"Sure." T.R. pulled several containers from the bottom of the box and then reached back for a spoon. The room began to fill with the aroma of coffee and toasted wheat bread with turkey slices.

T.R. set the food box on the table and slid a chair out as he sat down and pulled up a lid on the coffee. He began to drink then paused. "What kind of work are you in, Blake?"

"That's the problem." The man talked with food in his mouth. "I work for the IRS." He smiled. "Writing procedure manuals."

"That's why you're upset?" T.R. opened a sandwich and tore open a mustard package and he slid it across the bread.
Blake took another bite. "I hate the job—really. There are jerks everywhere. You can't get anything done. All the meetings, procedures and bubble heads with their own spin on everything."

"So, you're frustrated?"

"YOU BET."

"And you want something better."

"OF COURSE." He took more bites from the sandwich followed by loud slurping from the coffee.

T.R. lifted his own sandwich to his mouth and bit into it. "I assume you still want to write."

"Absolutely."

"Fiction?"

"Well, yeah," Blake began to calm. "Someday."

T.R. took a sip from his own coffee. "Well, your job is a

goldmine then."

"How you figure?"

"Look at all the great problems and people you can draw from now." T.R. took another bite of the sandwich. "That's the essence of great fiction."

Blake looked off in the distance as he chewed. "Never thought about it like that."

"I've had many jobs that I hated but later used in stories when I needed something bad to pull from."

"That so?"

T.R. nodded with another bite of his sandwich. "Nothing is ever wasted in life, Blake. You can always get another job."

Blake nodded again. He finished off the coffee.

"I can show you how to do all that." T.R. lifted a fruit bowl and fork and handed it over. "We can go over that later. But not if you're in a jail cell."

"What do you mean?"

"Well," he pointed the sandwich at Blake's box, "if that really is a bomb then you're holding two people hostage with some potential charges that could tie up several years." He raised both eyebrows. "But if we were to take you back to the hospital, then no one was harmed. You'd just spend another couple of days in the behavior unit, and you could go on with that great writing career I could help you with."

Blake pulled the lid off the fruit bowl and looked down in thought. "Might have a point there."

"It really was wrong of you to bust in here and terrorize Sara like this."

Blake nodded again with his eyes down.

"But I bet she'd over-look all this being the big-hearted professional that she is."

Blake looked up. "Think so?"

"Sure." He got up with his sandwich half eaten. "Give me that box." He extended his hands as Blake thought a moment then slowly lifted it toward him.

T.R. tossed the bomb into the empty container on the table that came from the café. Then he walked over to Sara's bedroom and knocked.

"WHAT DO YOU WANT?"

"Blake, here has something he wants to tell you."

The door flew open. Sara stood in her room in jeans and a white knit shirt. Her hand had a brush and was pulling it through her blonde hair. "What?"

Blake looked down again and held his hands together. "I'm sorry."

She laughed. "For what?"

"The bomb. Breaking in."

T.R. looked up. "He gave it to me and wants us to take him back to the hospital."

"Just like that?" she laughed again. "You virtually kidnap us with the intent to commit murder and now want the easy way out."

Blake looked down, hands in his pockets, surgical cap pulled low. "Guess it was the wrong way to get help."

"YOU GUESS!" Sara let both hands rise and then pointed her comb. "THERE ARE SOME THINGS YOU JUST DON'T DO."

"Like break in her house," T.R. added in a whisper. "And bring a bomb. Not good."

Blake looked up at both. "Sor-ry again."

T.R. took a deep breath and bent over to lift the box. "Well, let's get moving. We've got to take him back and get you to the radio station."

Sara put both hands on her waist. "When did you take over?"

"I'm just trying to help."

She pointed a finger at both. "I've had all I can take of you two."

T.R. started to back up. "Guess that means you'll ride with me, Blake."

Sara followed with her finger still outstretched. "I'm not done with you either."

Blake moved toward the door behind T.R. while both backed up the hall with Sara taking one step for each that they moved back.

"So, you were going to play your little game and let good ole Dr. Aspen teach you about love while the listening public trailed along."

"I really meant it," T.R. said.

She poked at the box in his arms. It made a depression in the side. "And when were you going to let me in on this?"

He stumbled and lifted his shoulders as he backed out the door. "Real soon."

"So what did you learn there, Mr. Romance?"

"I really didn't mean any harm," He slipped on the doorstep and backed into bushes as he continued up the walkway. "You're upset now. But think about it. We weren't ready for that anything real yet."

She raised her eyebrows. "That so?"

T.R. glanced down at the watch on Sara's wrist. "Are you coming? We only have several minutes to get you back to the station."

She shook her head. "So you can humiliate me some more with your experiment?"

"No." He stopped. "Your listeners really care. They want to hear you. They deserve that much."

Sara stopped and looked down. There was hurt in her eyes.

"No." She said with a look out at the horizon. "Not anymore. I've got to make some changes. This is as good a time as any."

"What about the show? You can't leave them hanging."

She lifted her eyebrows again. "Like you did with me?"

T.R. exhaled and started to turn away. "Please don't do that to them. Give your notice for later in the week. But at least meet the deadline today."

Sara looked down and there was a leveling in her eyes. "Then you do it."

"You don't mean that."

"Sure I do." She turned and started back into the condo. "You wreck my reputation with some public game about romance, so go on, finish the job."

He stood there and watched her walk off and shut the door.

~ * ~

T.R. threw the box into the back of the truck and drove fast to the station. The tires squealed around corners with Blake holding on to the door and the dog struggling to balance in the back. There was only one car when they pulled in. T.R. got out and ran into the building while Blake followed behind in his doctor's uniform.

He could hear Max shouting from inside the building.

"WHERE IS SHE?"

"Not coming."

"WHAT?"

"Told me to take her place."

"THAT SO?"

"Well." T.R. paused as Blake entered the waiting room. All three looked up at the clock on the wall. They had two minutes before the show started.

"Give us a chance," T.R. added. "I know the format. She presents a topic and the callers provide feedback."

"Okay." Max waited.

"Tonight's topic is…" T.R. looked at Blake, "problems at the workplace and we have an expert here to help."

He lifted a hand in Blake's direction. Max watched with no expression.

"Doctor?" he asked.

"Nope."

"Nurse?"

T.R. pointed at the clock and pulled open the door that led up the hallway for the sound booth. "He's with the IRS. Talk about great material for mental illness."

Max glanced at the clock also and pulled his mouth tight. "Whatever. We'll wing it."

They followed Max into the sound booth as he explained the process.

"What about the intro?" Max sat down behind his computer and lifted some head phones on. "Sara always did that on her own."

"Tell me her tagline and I'll modify it," T.R. said.

Max scribbled the words and handed over an index card. He pointed at the computer in front of them and the microphone overhead.

"You'll hear everything through the phones," he explained. "Watch the computer screen for caller names. Speak in a normal tone and watch my way for directions about time." He leaned back at the light on the wall. "Green means we're on and red goes into autopilot for commercials."

"Got it."

"This is basically a 20-minute local feature," Max added and looked up at the clock. "We're on in 30 seconds."

"Sounds good." T.R. lifted a pair of ear phones and sat down. Blake pulled up a chair and also put on a head set.

Max lifted ten fingers and began to pull the fingers down. T.R. scanned the index card and took a deep breath. The light turned green on the wall as theme music came over the speakers.

"Welcome to Mental Health and You. I'm T.R. Stallion in for Dr. Sara Aspen and tonight's topic is work-related stress." He paused. "We'll take your calls in a minute but first I want to introduce tonight's guest. He's an expert on mental health issues in the work setting. We'll call him Joe to protect his identity. Welcome to the show, Joe."

"Glad to be here."

"Joe works for a local government agency so we're not using his real name."

"I appreciate that," Blake said.

T.R. paused. "We were talking before the show about the kind of stress you see in co-workers."

"Got that right. Name the illness and I can match faces."

T.R. smiled. "What is it about government work that brings

out the worst in people?"

"I've wondered that a lot myself."

"For those of you who don't know me, I write romance novels," T.R. confessed. "Dr. Aspen was brave enough to let me take her place tonight. Writers have their own quirks. But Joe, tell us about some of the struggles you face on your job."

"The worst comes out in time management," he said. "That and meetings. For some odd reason, government agencies are full of time traps."

T.R. smiled. "You hit on something big. Our computer screen is filling up with callers." He looked up at Max. "Let's take one from a woman named Julie."

Static came over the speakers. "Hello, Julie—you're on. Welcome to our show."

"Yeah, thanks for taking my call," the woman started. "I work for the state government in an office and I can't get anything done with all the meetings. They call us together for stupid things like to announce someone's birthday."

"Let me take a guess," Blake suggested. "Then you get blamed for not doing your work."

"Right." Her voice got louder. "And I take it home where my husband and family can't understand why I'm up late to fill out the paperwork that should have been done in the office."

Blake looked over at T.R. "Julie's story could apply to many across our city."

"So what would you suggest?" T.R. asked.

"Julie have you voiced any of your concerns to supervisors?" Blake waited.

The woman began to talk fast. "THEY DON'T LISTEN."

Max adjusted the volume.

"They just talk at us," Julie added. "Ever been around people like that?"

"Yeah, I have," T.R. said. He let his eyes drift out the windows toward the river.

~ \* ~

Sara was looking at the same scene up the hill in her condo. The apartment was dark, the radio was on. And her thoughts scrambled to fill the gap between voices.

*You overreacted.*

*In what way?* she snapped. Voices continued on the radio with Blake sounding like an expert and T.R. leading the discussion. One part of her mind was there in the control booth as she imagined Max raising some fingers to announce a commercial break.

Another part of her tugged at her awareness like an objective counselor who wanted to be heard.

*He didn't mean any harm,* the voice said.

*Which one?* she responded in her mind. *The one with the bomb or the idiot with his romance game?*

*T.R...It was a harmless experiment.*

*Easy for you to say,* Sara imagined herself arguing.

*Look at you,* the counselor said inside her imagination. They were in her office, with the counselor in one chair and her in the other. But the face was missing on the listener.

*Notice the pattern,* the counselor continued. *Over-exaggerated reactions. Distorted thoughts.*

"What are you trying to say?" Sara asked out loud?

The lights were off in her living room; the city still laid out below the window in sparkling lights and the radio was still on with T.R. responding to another call.

The voice continued inside her. But the tone was soothing—just like she would have done if someone came to her in that state.

*You're tired,* the counselor replied from within. *Your feelings are raw and full of hurt.*

*So you're saying the problem is internal.*

*Maybe so.*

*As if I just need some rest and a good meal?*

The counselor paused inside her. *Emotions are hard to translate. They have a language all their own.*

*But I feel upset,* Sara told the voice inside.

*And don't deny that. Look at what you've been through recently.*

The music came on in the background radio with T.R. thanking everyone for listening.

"A special thanks for Dr. Sara Aspen," he added. "We love you doctor. Take care everybody. Have a good weekend. Goodnight."

"Love?" She looked at the lights again below her in the distance. "Does he even know what it means?"

*Lighten up,* the voice said within. *He's just being nice. Why get so anal about everything?*

*But I can't.*

*Everyone isn't like your dad.*

"Where did that thought come from?" she asked out loud.

*Really,* the voice said from within. *Everyone doesn't abandon their families.*

*So we're back to self analysis?* Sara asked within and got up in a slow groan. *I can't get away from this job—even in my thought life.*

She started into her bedroom and imagined herself with some late night reading before a good night's rest. But she looked down and saw two paperbacks on the bedside table. Both had T.R.'s name on the front.

"No way," she whispered. "I've got to deal with this now. Otherwise I never will."

She reached for her car keys and purse and started out of the house.

~ * ~

The cafe parking lot was empty except for a truck near the door. An old dog was in the back and Sara felt a smile appear as she walked up. His tail started to wag slowly and his eyes drifted into the building where his master sat at the bar alone.

The door was unlocked and Sara opened it.

"Just do a quick once-over," T.R. shouted. He had a cup of coffee in front of him and he didn't look up. "Don't worry about the deep cleaning tonight fellows."

She continued to walk toward him, her running shoes making squishy sounds, her jeans tight-legged, white knit shirt tucked. T.R. had his coffee cup to his lips when he looked over. He choked and set it down.

"Well hello." He got up.

She sat down beside him. "Just wanted to say—I'm sorry."

*There you go. Running into his arms as if you're the one who did something wrong.*

*So what do you suggest?* She argued with the voice inside her. *Hide the rest of my life and forget the facts?*

The shock melted in his expression. It was the look of recognition as if pulling elements together in his mind. He started back around the counter. "Let me get you a..."

"Decaf. I've missed enough sleep."

He nodded and reached for a cup and the pot on the burner. Sara watched his movements.

"Where's the expert?"

T.R. smiled. "Back at the hospital. They were glad to get him."

"I listened to the program." She smiled. "Sounded great."

"Thanks." He set the cup down in front of her and pulled some containers of sugar and cream over and reached for a spoon.

She watched him, eyes taking in his movements and form. He had a grace of movement that athletes use. It was just beyond her awareness like the feelings that were stirring within her.

"I really don't think he meant any harm," T.R. added, his eyes down as he came back around the counter and sat down. "He just wanted someone to—listen."

"And you?" She reached for a cup and lifted it to her lips. It had layers of steam that floated up with a smell like caramel.

"Sorry if I embarrassed you," he glanced over and then

looked down with a deep breath. "It just came over me."

"What?"

"These feelings." He looked over again and smiled. "Started the moment I saw you and only got worse."

"Is that bad?" She sipped again.

He leaned back and put his arm around the back of her chair, his heart beginning to pick up speed. "I was being honest that first day on the radio when I said that I really don't understand love." He looked up. "That's why this has been almost surreal." His expression was little-boy like. "It started with curiosity. Academic interest. Detached emotions." He smiled. "Sounds nice, right? Nice and safe." He took another long pull from the coffee cup. "Then I see you and my world turns upside down."

His eyes dropped.

"In what way?"

"I've been writing about romance for years now. And for some unknown reason women respond… but I never experienced that helplessness—till now."

He looked at her again, his brown eyes taking in everything. "It only got worse as we started talking." He inhaled a deep breath. "This desire grew—to know and be with you. Here people expect me to understand love but I have no idea."

She could feel it—all in a glance, a vulnerability that loosened everything inside her. She began to relax.

"I really don't understand women," he whispered. "Or love. It's my own private hell where I pretend on paper and people watch."

"This is hard for you to say." Her blue eyes looked into his. They both leaned closer to each other. The pause drew them, their eyes open and full of weakness.

T.R. eased his lips closer to hers. They almost touched when the door to the café opened with a bang. Both heads turned and several college students entered with mop buckets and a big radio.

"Sorry," one said. "Want us to come back?"

"No." T.R. got up. "We're in your way.' He pulled Sara's

chair back. "Want to sit out on the deck?"

She got up with a smile. "You mean with the blankets?"

"No… I mean yes."

"Sure, but not to sleep out there." She looked over at the students. They were looking back. "I fell asleep talking with him out there the other night."

"Hey, don't mind us," one of them answered.

T.R. pointed at the door. Sara looked through the windows at the river, now dark with the lights of the city rolling over the surface. She got up and followed him through the cafe.

Sea gulls cried in the distance. A tug approached from down river with a small wake in front as the bow pushed onward.

T.R. stood off to the side and held the door open as they stepped on to the deck. Wind caught their hair with a soft edge that was both cold and hot.

"The knife edge of seasons," he whispered.

She moved closer. "How's that?"

"Some people call it Indian summer, but I used to see it as the currents of time that could flow one way or the other."

He walked beside her as they watched the water. It rippled in swells from the tug and barge.

She smiled. "Grow up here?"

"Some." He looked down as if self conscious. "My parents wandered a lot."

She waited with an awareness that was just below the surface.

*Non-verbal change*, a voice said within. *He's tense, expressions stiff.*

"What difference does it make," she whispered.

"What's that?" T.R. looked down.

Sara smiled as if caught. "Talking to myself."

He put both hands in his pockets and shifted balance to look down at her.

*There again*, she told herself. *Awkward movements. Sudden stiffening.*

She pulled away. "Forgive me."

"For what?"

"The process I can't stop in my head." She breathed deeply and closed her eyes. "A classification system that collates your words and looks for a pattern."

She eased closer as if to ignore the feedback. "I don't want to be a counselor right now."

He noticed her eyes. "You can't get away from who you are."

She met the gaze. "So tell me about your family."

"They weren't the average types with a career." He looked down at the water. "We came on a sailboat and stopped at the waterfront."

"So that's where 'bend in the road' came in?"

"Sure." he stepped closer then stopped, eyes still on the water. "They built this out of a warehouse."

"Past tense?"

"That's the difficult part. I grew up on the water. That meant learning to sail early." He stopped and smiled at the thought. "We went all over the hemisphere. But they later..."

She looked up at his eyes. "Something bad happened?"

"Sailed out one day and never came back."

"Any trace?"

"Coast Guard found wreckage." He let his eyes pass over the river again. "Small chunks of the deck and hull, but no word on them."

"What did they suspect?"

"An explosion."

"As in bomb?"

"No," he said looking down river. "Tanker or big ship."

Sara let the wind carry hair off to the side and pulled it out of her eyes. "As in collision at sea?"

"Big ships don't always notice everything—especially a small sailboat drifting around at night."

"Wow."

He looked in her eyes again. "That counselor mind is

spinning fast now."

"When did it happen?"

"When I was in college."

"What about girlfriends? Anyone special?"

"I knew this was coming."

Sara stopped. Her eyes searched his. "You don't want to talk about this."

"More like can't."

"That painful?"

He pursed his lips. "She died."

"You were married?"

"Engaged."

"What happened?" She lifted a hand. "Don't answer that if you don't want to."

"No that's okay." He stopped again. "It's been a while."

He glanced at the railing. "Food poisoning."

Both were silent now. T.R. looked up at her eyes as if to catch the drift of her thoughts. "So what's the diagnosis?"

Sara squinted as if pulled from a day dream. "That's a lot to carry all these years."

T.R. pointed up at the second floor of the cafe. "That's why I started with fiction." He nodded with his head. "Want to see?"

Sara had question marks in her eyes and nodded slowly as he led to steps up the side of the building. He opened the door and turned on the light. Sara walked in and let her eyes wander.

One wall was a series of windows from floor to ceiling. They faced the river with a desk pulled back as if to watch. Behind it was a wall made of soft wood paneling. Frames held pictures and old book covers. An old leather couch rested along the wall. The floor was hardwood and clean with thick layers of varnish.

Sara nodded as she entered. A lap top remained on the desk but no papers. Everything was neat, in order and straight.

"You stay up here?" she asked.

"Sometimes."

She let her fingers drag across the desk. A door opened at the end of the room. She let her eyes pull her there and flipped a switch. It was a bathroom with new fixtures, folded towels off to the side and even the soap and aftershave bottles arranged in neat rows.

"The psychologist in me wants to catalog these details." She turned and met his gaze. "But I won't."

Dark water glimmered off to the side. It came from the wake of a sailboat just below the windows. The sloop was under power in a push up river, bow rising in the dark liquid, skiff in tow behind it. T.R. reached for the wall switch and pulled it down. The room was dark but the water bent shafts of light and sent them into the loft with angles that wiggled.

Sara walked closer to the windows.

"I'm speechless," she said.

"I spend days up here."

"I would love that...." She turned and felt his presence, strong, sure, peaceful. "It's that place inside me I always wanted to go."

He was close to her, close enough to feel her breathing. "Great, cause I can't do this anymore."

Her eyelids pulled half shut. "Do what?"

"Dream. Work. Live in my head." He pulled her close and felt the arms tighten around his waist. The sailboat now was just below them with rigging and masts that filled their window as they passed.

Some voices came from below. It was the cleaning crew on their way to the dumpster. T.R. saw them pass below with boxes and large bags of trash.

Sara heard the shouts and turned, her eyes on the sailboat with moon on the water. They pulled closer in a slow embrace.

One of the voices shouted over the others below. "Hey, what's that box in the boss's truck? I'll get it."

T.R. let his eyes drift at the shadow below them and heard the dumpster open as the box hurled over the top and inside.

Fire shot upward. A flash followed behind as dumpster parts tumbled skyward. The three janitors rolled back on the pavement with shock as the force passed them in a wave. All three then looked back up at the windows as T.R. looked down at them.

"That's crazy," one of the janitors snapped. "What did you have in that box?"

T.R. looked out at the boxes and paper floating across the parking lot and then at the shock in Sara's eyes.

"Blake wasn't kidding," he said to her. "It really was a bomb."

Both smiled as they moved slowly together.

"I'm crazy 'bout you," he whispered.

# Time Changes

Nicolette Zamora

The tiny café was packed with people trying to beat the hustle and grab a quick coffee before getting back to their weekends. Laurie Palson watched as two guys laughed and joked as they waited, both seemingly happier than Laurie had been in a long time.

"Earth to Laurie," Meg called, waving a hand in Laurie's face.

"Sorry," Laurie said. She managed a weak smile. "I just never realized how hard breaking up with someone is. I had always thought that being the dumpee would be easier."

"Well," Meg drawled, taking a long swig of her cappuccino "let's review why you dumped Derek in the first place. One, he was an arrogant pig."

"Not always. He just didn't always think about others first."

"What about that time when he left you alone at a wedding so that he could watch football? It's not as if he couldn't tape the game. And he was never on time to pick you up, he never called, after dating for a year still hadn't brought you home to meet the 'rents, maybe hadn't even told them about you."

"We did have some good times together," Laurie protested.

"I thought we were talking about why you finally decided to dump him."

"I know. It's just that you're making it sound really awful that I was with him as long as I was," Laurie sighed. She had broken up with Derek a week ago, an impulsive act, right after he had flaked on their Valentine's Day plans for a hockey game with the guys.

"Laurie, when was the last time you had fun with a guy?" Meg leaned forward, her chocolate hair falling over her shoulder despite her ponytail. Her normally twinkling green eyes were unusually serious.

Laurie thought for a moment before answering. Then it hit her: Gary. Her high school sweetheart. They had been perfect for each other, she had believed at the time, always having fun and enjoying each other. He listened to her hopes, dreams, and shared his goals too. And therein was the problem: he had gone to a college in Pennsylvania for a physician assistant program whereas Laurie had stayed in Slaterville Springs, a quaint little town in upstate New York. Laurie's grandmother had been her constant companion, more like an older sister or another motherly figure, and her recent diagnosis of cancer propelled Laurie to choose a school much closer to home. So Laurie and Gary had broken up, not wishing to try a long distance relationship, not when college meant so much to them and Laurie worrying about her grandmother. And when her grandmother had died during Laurie's sophomore year, she knew that she had made the right decision by staying. She had never regretted the break up as much as she did now.

"Since high school." Laurie said quietly.

Meg, her Ithaca college roommate, had heard all about Gary. Knowing the non-possibility that was, Meg said, "You know my motto. It's better to try out lots of fish before going after the king." Easy enough for Meg to say, she had new boyfriends every month.

Meg glanced around the café. "How 'bout that guy? He looks cute."

Laurie spotted the man right away. He stood next to the napkin holder and watched as a little girl reached up for some. Much too short, she merely looked at the man and her face broke out into an enormous toothless grin as he handed her several.

Laurie couldn't help but smile at the sight.

Suddenly, the man in question looked in the direction of their table, as if he heard them talking about him, and gave Laurie the small, nearly non-existence smile that strangers give each other. He patted the little girl on the head and walked out. Could it be? It looked just like him… Rob Hender? Gary's twin brother?

"Now that is a man that thinks of others," Meg said with a sigh. "Perfect for you. Now you just have to haunt this joint until he shows up again and…"

Laurie wasn't paying attention. She pulled on her curly blond hair, a nervous habit she had developed when visiting her grandmother in the hospital. Maybe she could hunt down Rob. But her thoughts weren't on Rob, they were on Gary. If Rob was in the area, maybe Gary wasn't too far off. *I wonder how he's doing after all these years.* Her heart began to race and she barely tasted her cream laced coffee. Rob had a much more football player build. Gary had been skinner, his muscles not as outwardly visible. Both were tall, around six feet, with dark hair and eyes. Laurie still remembered the last time she had stroked Gary's face, when they had agreed that parting was their best choice.

Meg stood up, a broad grin on her face. "I'll leave you to your daydreams," Meg teased. "I'm sure I'll be seeing you 'round here a lot more often." With a wink, she dropped her empty cup into the trashcan before leaving.

~ * ~

Eight days later, Laurie finally saw Rob at the coffee shop again. She sat by the entrance and noticed him as soon as he entered the place. She waited until he received his order and was about to leave before waving him over. Laurie opened her mouth but didn't have the chance to speak because he exclaimed, "Laurie? Is that really you?"

Laurie's jaw dropped. From the front, she realized that she had been wrong. This man wasn't Rob; it was Gary! A much more handsome Gary, with huge biceps, the reason why she had assumed he was his brother. But his eyes were the same twinkling stars and his voice was just as deep and husky as she remembered.

Her shock and confusion left her tongue-tied and twisted, with nothing to say and too shy and unnerved to look him in the face. Exactly as she had been on their first date—how there had been a second one, she had never been able to fathom. All week she had longed to talk to his brother so that this reunion could take place, but she had imagined that she would be able to prepare first!

Finally, she gave him a timid smile and gestured for him to sit. "Do you have time to catch up with an old friend?" Laurie asked, finally finding her voice, amazed that it wasn't shaking.

Gary had already sat down. "Wow, o wow. You look great,

Laurie."

"I thought you were Rob!" Laurie blurted out.

"Thanks. I know all the girls in school used to drool over his arms."

Laurie blushed. She had been one of the few to overlook Rob; she had always only had eyes for Gary. "So what brings you to the neighborhood?"

"Trying to find a place to stay."

"Moving back here?"

"Yes. Pennsylvania's a great state but is excessively overpopulated with assistants. I have several job interviews lined up, all with pay rates much higher than I would get in PA. I'm crashing with Rob until I find a place."

"Wow, that's great. I never thought that you would move back to the area."

"I didn't think I would either." Gary shrugged. "But I'm finding that I don't mind. Not much has changed."

"Naw, it'll always be the same here." Laurie bit her lip, wishing she had something more significant to say.

"So what have you been up to?" Gary leaned back on his chair, taking a long swig of his drink.

"I teach algebra at our high school."

"Wonderful. I'm so glad to hear that you made your dreams come true."

Not all of them, she thought wryly. She took a sip and noticed that his left hand sported no ring. He followed her gaze and chuckled. "No, no wife. Not yet at least. You?"

She grinned, suddenly feeling reckless. "No wife for me either."

He laughed. "Quick wit, as always. Boyfriend then?"

A toss of her blond hair from side to side as she shook her head. "Currently single. I just recently broke up with someone."

"Well, I was just dumped." He sighed. "Romance just isn't fun and games anymore. Not like it used to be." He sounded bitter, something that Laurie would have never before associated with him.

The Gary she remembered was carefree, a wild spirit with a passion for life. Laurie was suddenly aware that this Gary was all grown up, a different person from the one she had dated, with scars and memories that she wasn't privy to. Not like before. And she also wasn't the same young girl from high school. She was more mature now, with a job and a place of her own. The time spent with her grandmother had made her appreciate family, something that Gary and young Laurie had never talked about. She certainly was still attracted to him, which remained despite the passing of years, but she no longer knew his hopes and wishes, desires and fears. The man in front of her wore a familiar face but was still a stranger.

Laurie smiled again, wishing for the conversation to be lighter. "Maybe what's changed is what you want out of a relationship," she said airily.

"I guess you could say that," he said slowly. Laurie saw the gears grinding in his head.

She cleared her throat. She wasn't sure what to say and Gary had stopped talking as well. She could not believe how surreal this was! Talking to Gary again was a dream come true yet she couldn't find the words to keep the conversation going. They never used to have awkward, silent moments before.

"Time certainly can change a person," Gary finally said.

"For better or for worse," Laurie agreed.

Gary glanced at his watch and sighed. "I better get going. It was nice catching up with you."

Laurie managed a smile. They had hardly caught up at all.

Evidently her face displayed her disagreement and Gary laughed, the same easygoing laugh that she had fallen in love with. "All right, all right. So we had two minutes, if that. Not much time for a couple such as ourselves. We go back too far for that. How about one last date for old time's sake?"

"I'm willing," Laurie said at the same time that Gary finished:

"At least a dinner."

"What? Cheapskate, are we now? No movie? Heck, we could

even rent something and watch it at my place." Dinner and a movie had been their last official date. Most of their time spent together had been at the park or one of their parents' houses. They had been poor high schoolers, after all.

"Whatever you want," Gary promised.

Laurie gave him a bittersweet smile. "Remember the last time you said that to me?"

He nodded. "I wanted you to decide, for us, about us."

She grinned, lightening up the somber mood. "Well, now I want dinner and a movie."

He laughed and Laurie was glad to hear that it hadn't changed: a real, strong, hearty laugh that meant he was happy. "Okay, okay, dinner and a movie." He stressed the 'and.' "Where is your place?"

Laurie recited her address.

"And when?"

"I'm a school teacher. My life isn't too exciting," she said dryly, "whenever is fine."

"Then I'll pick you up tomorrow at four. Movie first?"

"Sounds good to me." She drained the last of her coffee and stood up. "I should get going, I have tests to grade."

"Go easy on them." He grimaced. "I never did do well in algebra."

Laurie smiled and waved good-bye as she left the shop behind. She was tempted to call Meg and ask for advice on what to wear when she shook her head. A date with Gary didn't mean that she should start acting like a high schooler again!

~ * ~

A movie may not have been the best of ideas, Laurie realized the next night. Sure, Gary sat beside her, his arm causally across the back of her seat, but there was no way to talk and the teenagers in front of them were making out. Plus, the movie wasn't that thrilling—it was a sequel of a mediocre movie, with a rehash of the same car chases and action sequences, with a fight between the main characters that would, of course, end with them back together again. When the lights finally came back on, Laurie turned to Gary. Before she could say anything, he sheepishly admitted, "Maybe next time, you can pick the movie."

"Oh no. Watching the same movie twice really isn't that bad. Of course, the first time around wasn't that great either." Laurie's heart thundered at the words 'next time' but she refused to allow herself to think about that. Now was all that mattered; it was time to rediscover who Gary was and whether or not she could still consider him a friend, let alone anything more than that.

They laughed and left the theatre. As Gary pulled out of the parking spot, he glanced over, a strange look on his face. "Is Italian still your favorite?"

"Yes," Laurie said. She straightened her black skirt and fixed her low cut blouse, just wishing to have something for her hands to do.

"Good. I made reservations at Joe's." Gary's face relaxed but he still seemed a little too tense, too uptight.

When they got to the restaurant, Gary held out Laurie's chair before sitting across from her. The candlelight made his strong features more rugged and Laurie could not remember a time when he looked handsomer. Well, prom was up there too.

"Why are you smiling?"

"I was just thinking about prom."

"Which one?"

"Both."

He returned the smile. "You certainly looked gorgeous that night. Er, those nights."

"And you were the handsomest man there."

"Were?"

Laurie laughed.

Their waiter came over. "Can I interest you in any wine this evening?"

Gary glanced at Laurie. He mouthed 'merlot' and she

7

nodded. "A bottle of merlot, please." He ordered and the waiter hurried away.

Gary laughed. "Sharing a bottle of wine with little Laurie. Never would have thought."

"We all have to grow up sometime." Laurie grinned. "Although it isn't as if this would be the first time we're having alcohol together."

Gary grinned. "A yeah, that can of beer. I thought you were gonna get sick."

"I still can't stand the taste of beer. It just rubs me the wrong way." She grimaced at the memory of bitter taste and repressed gag reflex. "We did get into our share of trouble."

"Yeah, our reputation was set when we fell asleep at the movie theater. Just like that Simon and Garfunkel song. Course that was probably the only time we were innocent."

Laurie laughed. Reminiscing was grand but she also wanted to find out more about adult Gary. She already knew everything about teen Gary. After they ordered their food and munched on delicious breadsticks, Laurie asked, "How was PA school? Was it everything you thought it would be?"

"It was rough. The undergrad part was easy enough but the master portion, crazy. All these different rotations and…"

As Gary told her all about his schooling, Laurie couldn't help but be proud. He had wanted to be a physician assistant since he had first learned what one was. His parents, neither of whom had gone to college, had not been the most supportive but Gary had not backed down from his dream. And now he was certified and ready to start his professional career. Laurie was so proud of him and she told him so.

"Thank you. I don't think I could have come this far without you. Even though we broke up, I still thought of you. Was actually a little worried about bumping into you around town."

"Worried?"

"I thought for sure that you would have found someone by now."

"Well, I didn't. I guess a certain someone set the bar a little too high out of reach," she teased.

"I used to think that we would get married. But I was afraid to say anything. I mean, we were so young and I knew how much your grandmother meant to you and the best schools for me were in PA. We had to drift apart. And now it seems so surreal to be sitting across from you."

"It does, doesn't it? Like a dream that you could wake up from at any moment."

"Little Laurie. All grown up. I don't even know you anymore," he said sadly.

"It's true; we aren't the same people we used to be..."

"Do you know, I reserved all different kinds of restaurants. I wanted to take you wherever was your favorite, only I wasn't sure if your tastes had changed."

"That's really touching," Laurie said, a slow blush forming on her cheeks.

"Or ridiculous," he muttered before clasping his hands and his eyes turning brighter. "Tell me everything about you: your dreams, your favorite color, everything. I want to know the now Laurie. See if she's anything at all like the past."

"Only if you'll tell me..." She gestured with her hands, back and forth.

"Of course."

"Well, I still love red."

"The color of passion."

She grinned. "I may be an algebra teacher but I've been thinking about writing lately."

"You want to be an author? What kind of stories?"

"Young adult mostly. But although I have many ideas, I haven't finished one manuscript yet."

"I wouldn't mind reading what you have so far."

Laurie hesitated. She hadn't let anyone read her writing. In fact, not many people knew that she did in the first place. But Gary seemed so earnest and some feedback would help. "All right."

She sighed. "Let's see." She didn't have to tell him about her grandmother's passing, she had already told him via the only letter correspondence between the two during college. "The reason why I broke up with my last boyfriend was because we never had any fun, he was much too serious, and we just didn't... connect. We spent time together but it wasn't as if we actually.... We just didn't talk about things that mattered. We didn't care about each other. Not enough, anyway. So we parted ways."

"Ah, the old flames. Well, Alice was one of my classmates. Type A personality which should have been a warning flag. She always was studying, worrying about her grades. I cared about my grades too, but I wanted to learn more from an application standpoint. She just cared about the letter grade. Well, we were in a study group together and sometimes would be the only two to show up so it only seemed natural to ask her out. We did get along for the most part but she was just too uptight all the time. And she wasn't very supportive of me when the incident happened."

"What incident?"

"Well, a bunch of the guys were playing soccer. It was all fun and games until I got kicked, hard, in the groin. Had to go to the hospital, was the most embarrassing moment in my life. They had to run a bunch of tests and actually had to remove one testicle. From all the testing, they found out that I'm sterile."

"My God, Gary, I'm so sorry," Laurie gasped, her hand on her throat.

"Yeah, well, Alice, perfect Alice, wanted a large house with a white picket fence and two point five kids. Couldn't exactly promise her that, now then, could I? And she wasn't sympathetic either about the whole thing. Thought I was immature for playing, let alone getting hurt." He sighed and rubbed his eyes. "So, she wanted more from me than I could give and I had to get out. Leave."

"You never ran from relationships before," Laurie wondered aloud, "not even ours."

"That's because things were different with Alice. I never could see myself with her long term." He paused, opening and closing his mouth, as if willing himself to say something. He stared at her, his eyes turning darker. He took a long swig from his wine glass and Laurie realized it was for courage when he blurted out, "Did you ever blame me for us breaking up?"

Laurie's eyes widened. She had not expected that at all. "No!" She protested.

"I... a part of me always regretted it," Gary said, staring at the red liquid in front of him.

"Regretted what?"

"That we didn't even try. A long distance relationship, I mean."

"Did you have any friends freshman year that had a girl back home?"

"A couple," Gary nodded.

"And did any work out?"

He shook his head.

"What makes you think that we would have been any different?" Laurie asked softly.

"But we could have tried. We should have tried. I thought about you constantly and after all the time we spent together, we just threw it all away because of miles!"

Laurie was struck by his bitter and unhappy tone. His dark eyes were stormy and Laurie's heart melted.

"Well, maybe fate is trying to tell us something. After all these years, we happen to run into each other when we're both single. We could give us another shot, now that we're in the same city again."

"I've been looking for jobs all over the place. Some might be easier for me if I didn't live here in town," Gary warned. Despite his words, Laurie was almost certain that his eyes were hopeful.

"You're not the same person you were in high school. Time changes people, for better and for worse." She reiterated their words from the previous day. "It might be just as well that you might not be staying in town for long," Laurie said, her words piercing her heart as she voiced them. Oh, how she longed to be with him again!

But she had to remember that he was a changed man now, with more cause for anger and resentment, two things that Laurie never would have associated with the carefree, fun-loving Gary of old. Despite this obvious change, Laurie still felt certain that they, at the very least, would always be friends. She damn well wanted to give it another go.

"Or I might have a reason to stick around. We'll just have to wait and see." Gary smiled, a light came over his face, and Laurie could practically see how peaceful and happy he was for what was probably the first time in awhile. She was determined to keep that light shining on him.

~ * ~

Gary could not remember the last time that he felt so content. Eating dinner with his high school sweetheart, good food, quiet atmosphere, the night was going really well. Although he couldn't believe that he had already confided his infertility to her, Gary knew that he still wanted to share everything with the gorgeous woman in front of him.

I always thought she was beautiful, but now... wow! Gary could not believe the quiet grace that Laurie now possessed. She had a dignity that she had lacked in high school. Her hair was falling from her bun and framed her face with soft curls. And her eyes, smoky gray, passionate... was it his imagination or did they mirror the hope that he was feeling too?

Gary hadn't come back to town to find a wife. He had needed a place to stay, far from Pennsylvania. And Alice. He needed a job. But if Laurie was right and fate was shoving them back together again....

Gary ate more of his chicken parmesan. The perfect blend of chicken and cheese and homemade sauce was delicious. Gary had never cared for Italian food until meeting Laurie. She had been such a huge influential part of his life and he now hoped that she always would be.

Yet one thing nagged him. He knew how much family meant to Laurie. After all, family was why they had broken up in the first place; she had needed to stay behind to spend the last few years of her grandmother's life with her. And Gary respected that. Admired it. Her spunk and determination were two of the reasons he had fallen in love with her in the first place. But now he could never give her a family of her own. And that bothered him as much as it would bother her, if she had even thought that far ahead.

Not that she should have. She was right; they were both different people now. But that didn't matter to him. He wanted to know all about her life, her time spent on earth when he hadn't been by her side. He wanted to spend the rest of his life with her; he now wondered how he could have ever left her side.

"The food is delicious," Laurie said softly, her eyes sparkling. Ever since their food had been served, the two had not spoken much, instead concentrating on the task at hand: enjoying the marvelous meal.

"Divine," Gary agreed. "Just like you." He reached across the table and gently held her hand. Her skin was just as smooth as it had been years ago and Gary's hand was burning. Her skin, her touch was more intoxicating than the two glasses of wine he had drank.

Laurie smiled, a gentle, teasing smile. Her cheeks were rosy and added to her beauty. She glanced away and Gary noticed her slender neck, snow white, innocent and pure.

"Should I be getting the young school teacher back to her place? Is it almost her curfew?"

She grinned, a reckless curve of her lips that sent Gary's heart for a loop and left him breathless. "I really should."

"May I see you again?"

"That depends." She tilted her head to the side and gave him a puzzling glance.

"Depends?" Any conditions, any terms... he would satisfy them.

"Would it still be for old time's sake?"

Gary just stared at her, at her beauty, at the woman that time had changed and matured. She may not be little Laurie anymore but she still had his heart captivated. "No." Gary cleared his throat. "No. For young time, new memories, old flames but new fire."

Laurie's face lit up and Gary smiled. He could just stare at her for hours. "Come on, let me take you home."

~ * ~

Chivalry wasn't completely dead. Gary held out her chair for her and walked her, arm-in-arm, to the car. She carried the bottle of wine, minus four glasses, as if it was a trophy for how well the night had gone. "I had such a great time," Laurie said, not caring that she was gushing. She felt as if nothing could harm her, nothing could cause the night to end other than perfectly.

Gary glanced over as he started the ignition. "So did I." He winked at her, that light on his face illuminating the car and Laurie leaned over and kissed him on the cheek. She could not be happier.

Or more tired. She yawned and Gary laughed. "Go ahead, close your eyes. I'll get you home safely."

"I'm fine, I'm fine." She yawned again. "It must be the wine."

He grinned and pulled out of the parking lot.

As the car sped along in the darkness, Laurie was tempted to close her eyes but she refused, instead wanting to enjoy just spending time with him. She glanced at his side profile and wanted to trace his jawbone, kiss his neck, and just be held by those strong arms.

Just then, Gary sat up straighter, his back rigid. Laurie glanced ahead and saw a car in the other lane bearing down on them, driving much too fast, skating across the center line. "Watch out!" she cried but there wasn't time for Gary to react and the two cars collided, head on.

~ * ~

Laurie woke up first. "Ga-ry?" she croaked, her throat so dry that the name hardly was pronounced.

"He's fine. Has a sore noggin' from his forehead hitting the windshield but other than that, he's just fine. You are too, just some bruises."

"And the other driver?" Laurie asked, glancing around. She saw Gary, his head wrapped in gauze, talking earnestly to another EMT and some police officers. He turned and smiled and waved when he saw her. Laurie smiled back and winced; her ribs were sore.

"From the seat belt. Just some bruises, like I said. It's a good thing that you both were wearing them." The EMT sighed. Maybe twenty years Laurie's senior, the lady was slightly plump but worked with ease and grace that belied her size. Laurie liked her immediately, but couldn't help but feel as though she was avoiding her question.

"The other driver?" Laurie asked again.

"Didn't make it," the woman said finally. Her dark eyes were furious. "Stupid moron. Should never have been out on the road. His blood alcohol level was nearly twice the legal amount! And he wasn't wearing a belt, let me tell you. Went right through the windshield and bounced off your car." She muttered to herself as she examined Laurie for any more bruises than her ribs. "I hate drunk drivers. Not only put themselves in trouble but everyone else too!"

Laurie smiled in agreement but glanced over at Gary. She was so relieved that he was all right. He mattered so much to her that she now knew that she could never be parted from him again. She had loved him once, had never truly stopped, and would always love him.

She had been silent during dinner, worrying about their future, if they should decide to have one. And Laurie had to confess that she had been selfish, wishing that Gary had never had his incident, that he could still sire children. But now, after their brush with death, Laurie knew that she just wanted to spend the rest of her life with him, as his wife, even if she could never be the mother of his children.

After what felt like an eternity, Gary came over to her and wrapped her in his arms. She felt searing pain through her ribs but the pain meant nothing, all that mattered was Gary.

"I couldn't avoid it," Gary whispered in her hair. "I would have hit a tree if I veered. It all happened so fast."

"Gary, it wasn't your fault."

He stared at her, at her light gray eyes so full of hope and love. His mouth found hers and their hearts spoke in the tongues of angels. "Marry me," he said when they finally needed to catch their breath. "I know I can't support us yet, I need a job, and I know I can't give you children..."

"There are plenty of jobs in the area," Laurie said, her voice husky. "We have all the time in the world to spend together, might as well use some of it to adopt."

Gary slowly got down on one knee; his sore and aching body did not agree with the movement. "I'll buy you the largest diamond you want. You pick the ring. Only marry me. Be my wife."

"Time won't ever part us again," Laurie said as she helped him to his feet. "Yes. Oh, yes, Gary!" They kissed again and Laurie knew that her happiness was with Gary, her high school sweetheart, her fiancé.

## VISIT OUR WEBSITE
## FOR THE FULL INVENTORY
## OF QUALITY BOOKS:

*http://www.roguephoenixpress.com*

# Rogue Phoenix Press
*Representing Excellence in Publishing*

**Quality trade paperbacks and downloads
in multiple formats,
in genres ranging from historical to contemporary romance,
mystery and science fiction.
Visit the website then bookmark it.
We add new titles each month!**

www.ingramcontent.com/pod-product-compliance
Lightning Source LLC
Chambersburg PA
CBHW051957220626
47052CB00004B/986